THE AEROSMURF

Peyo

THE AEROSMURF

A **SMURFS** GRAPHIC NOVEL BY *Peyo*

PAPERCUTZ™
NEW YORK

SMURFS GRAPHIC NOVELS AVAILABLE FROM PAPERCUTZ™

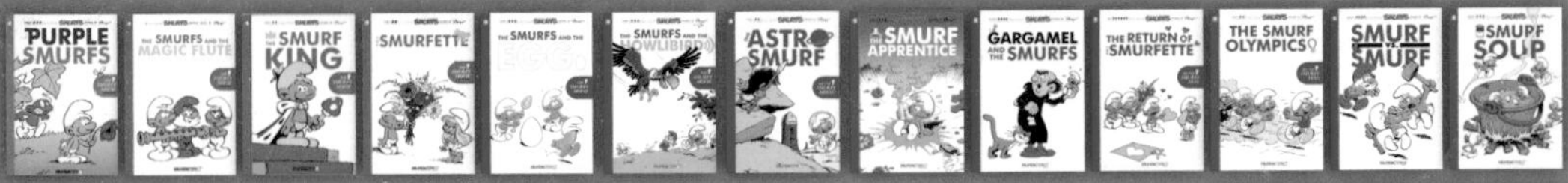
PURPLE SMURFS
THE SMURFS AND THE MAGIC FLUTE
THE SMURF KING
SMURFETTE
THE SMURFS AND THE EGG
THE SMURFS AND THE HOWLIBIRD
ASTRO SMURF
SMURF APPRENTICE
GARGAMEL AND THE SMURFS
THE RETURN OF SMURFETTE
THE SMURF OLYMPICS
SMURF VS SMURF
SMURF SOUP

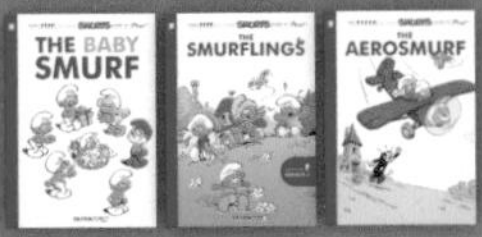
THE BABY SMURF
SMURFLINGS
AEROSMURF

1. **THE PURPLE SMURFS**
2. **THE SMURFS AND THE MAGIC FLUTE**
3. **THE SMURF KING**
4. **THE SMURFETTE**
5. **THE SMURFS AND THE EGG**
6. **THE SMURFS AND THE HOWLIBIRD**
7. **THE ASTROSMURF**
8. **THE SMURF APPRENTICE**
9. **GARGAMEL AND THE SMURFS**
10. **THE RETURN OF THE SMURFETTE**
11. **THE SMURF OLYMPICS**
12. **SMURF VS. SMURF**
13. **SMURF SOUP**
14. **THE BABY SMURF**
15. **THE SMURFLINGS**
16. **THE AEROSMURF**

COMING SOON:

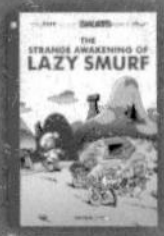
LAZY SMURF

17. **THE STRANGE AWAKENING OF LAZY SMURF**

THE SMURFS graphic novels are available in paperback for $5.99 each and in hardcover for $10.99 each at booksellers everywhere. You can also order online at www.papercutz.com. Or call 1-800-886-1223, Monday through Fridays, 9 – 5 EST. MC, Visa, and AmEx accepted. To order by mail, please add $4.00 for postage and handling for first book ordered, $1.00 for each additional book and make check payable to NBM Publishing. Send to: Papercutz, 160 Broadway, Suite 700, East Wing, New York, NY 10038.

THE SMURFS graphic novels are also available digitally wherever e-books are sold.

WWW.PAPERCUTZ.COM

THE AEROSMURF

"The Aerosmurf"
BY PEYO

"The Masked Smurf"
BY PEYO

"The Firesmurfs"
BY PEYO

"Gluttony and the Smurfs"
BY PEYO

"The Smurf and his Dragon"
BY PEYO

"Jokey Smurf's Pranks"
BY PEYO

Joe Johnson, *SMURFLATIONS*
Adam Grano, *SMURFIC DESIGN*
Janice Chiang, *LETTERING SMURFETTE*
Matt. Murray, *SMURF CONSULTANT*
Beth Scorzato, *SMURF COORDINATOR*
Michael Petranek, *ASSOCIATE SMURF*
Jim Salicrup, *SMURF-IN-CHIEF*

PAPERBACK EDITION ISBN: 978-1-59707-426-1
HARDCOVER EDITION ISBN: 978-1-59707-427-8

PRINTED IN CHINA AUGUST 2013 BY WKT CO. LTD.
3/F PHASE I LEADER INDUSTRIAL CENTRE
188 TEXACO ROAD, TSEUN WAN, N.T., HONG KONG

Papercutz books may be purchased for business or promotional use. For information on bulk purchases please contact Macmillan Corporate and Premium Sales Department at (800) 221-7945 x5442.

DISTRIBUTED BY MACMILLAN
FIRST PAPERCUTZ PRINTING

THE AEROSMURF

by Peyo

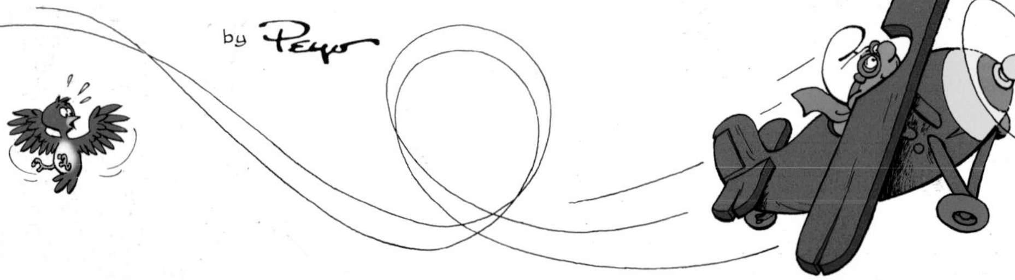

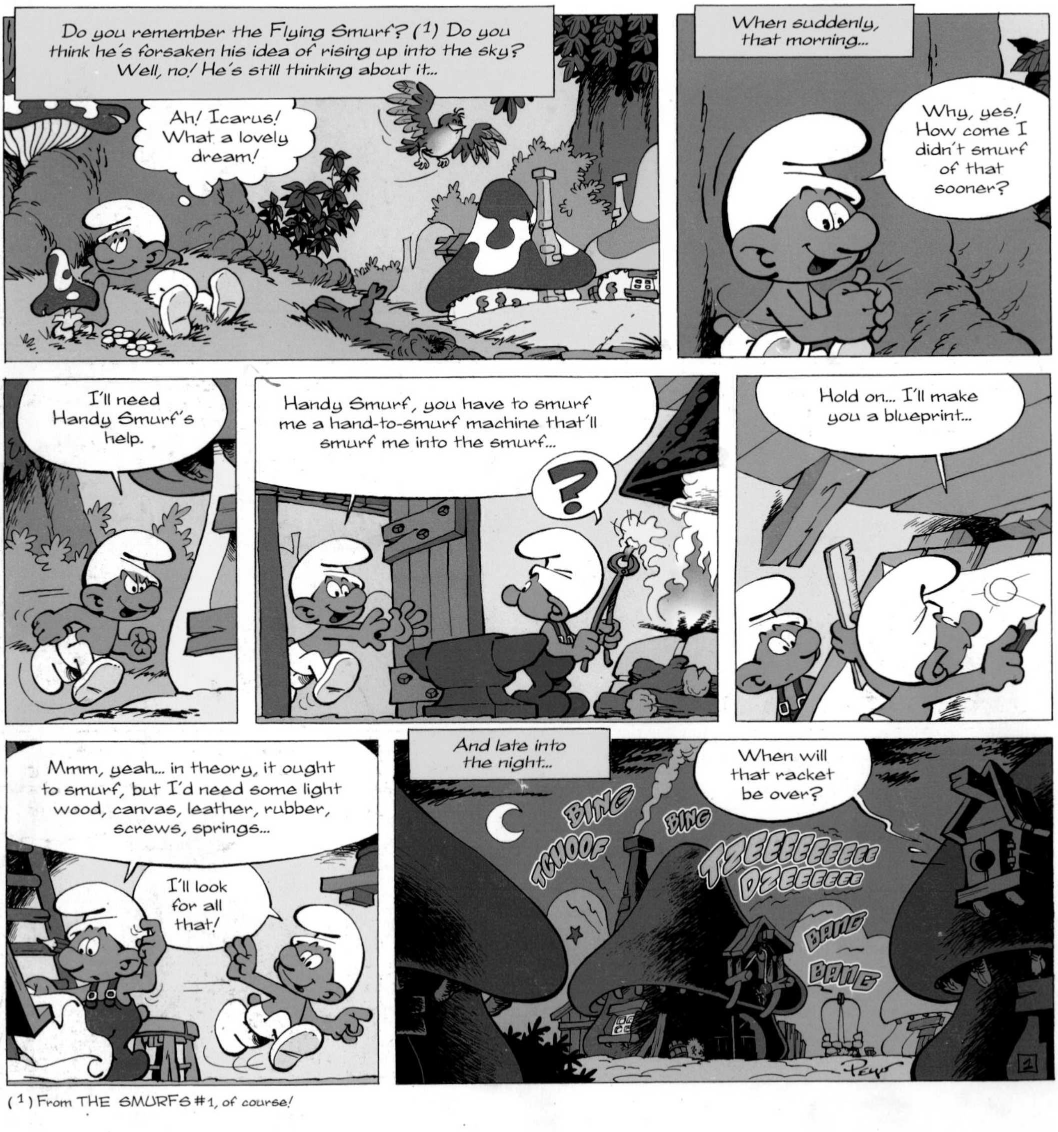

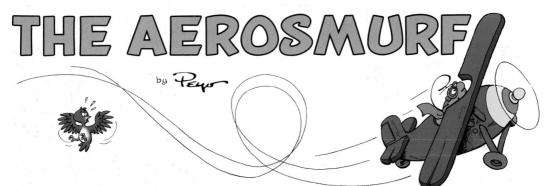

Do you remember the Flying Smurf? (1) Do you think he's forsaken his idea of rising up into the sky? Well, no! He's still thinking about it...
Ah! Icarus! What a lovely dream!
When suddenly, that morning...
Why, yes! How come I didn't smurf of that sooner?
I'll need Handy Smurf's help.
Handy Smurf, you have to smurf me a hand-to-smurf machine that'll smurf me into the smurf...
?
Hold on... I'll make you a blueprint...
Mmm, yeah... in theory, it ought to smurf, but I'd need some light wood, canvas, leather, rubber, screws, springs...
I'll look for all that!
And late into the night...
When will that racket be over?
BING
TCHOOF
BING
TZEEEEEEEEEE
DZEEEEEEE
BANG
BANG
Peyo
1

(1) From THE SMURFS #1, of course!

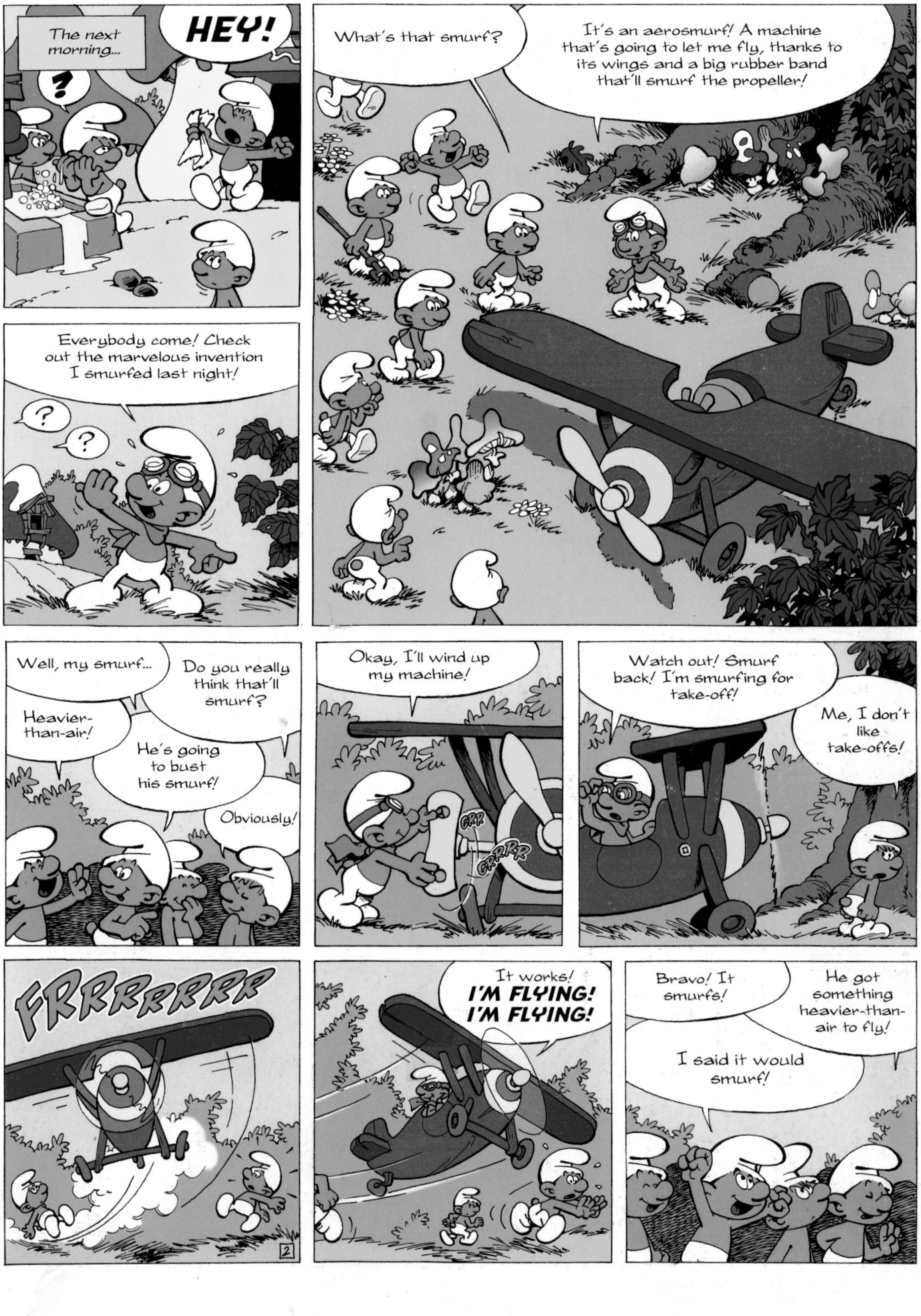
The next morning...
HEY!
?
What's that smurf?
It's an aerosmurf! A machine that's going to let me fly, thanks to its wings and a big rubber band that'll smurf the propeller!
Everybody come! Check out the marvelous invention I smurfed last night!
?
?
Well, my smurf...
Do you really think that'll smurf?
Heavier-than-air!
He's going to bust his smurf!
Obviously!
Okay, I'll wind up my machine!
GRR
GRRRR
Watch out! Smurf back! I'm smurfing for take-off!
Me, I don't like take-offs!
FRRRRRRR
2
It works! I'M FLYING! I'M FLYING!
Bravo! It smurfs!
He got something heavier-than-air to fly!
I said it would smurf!

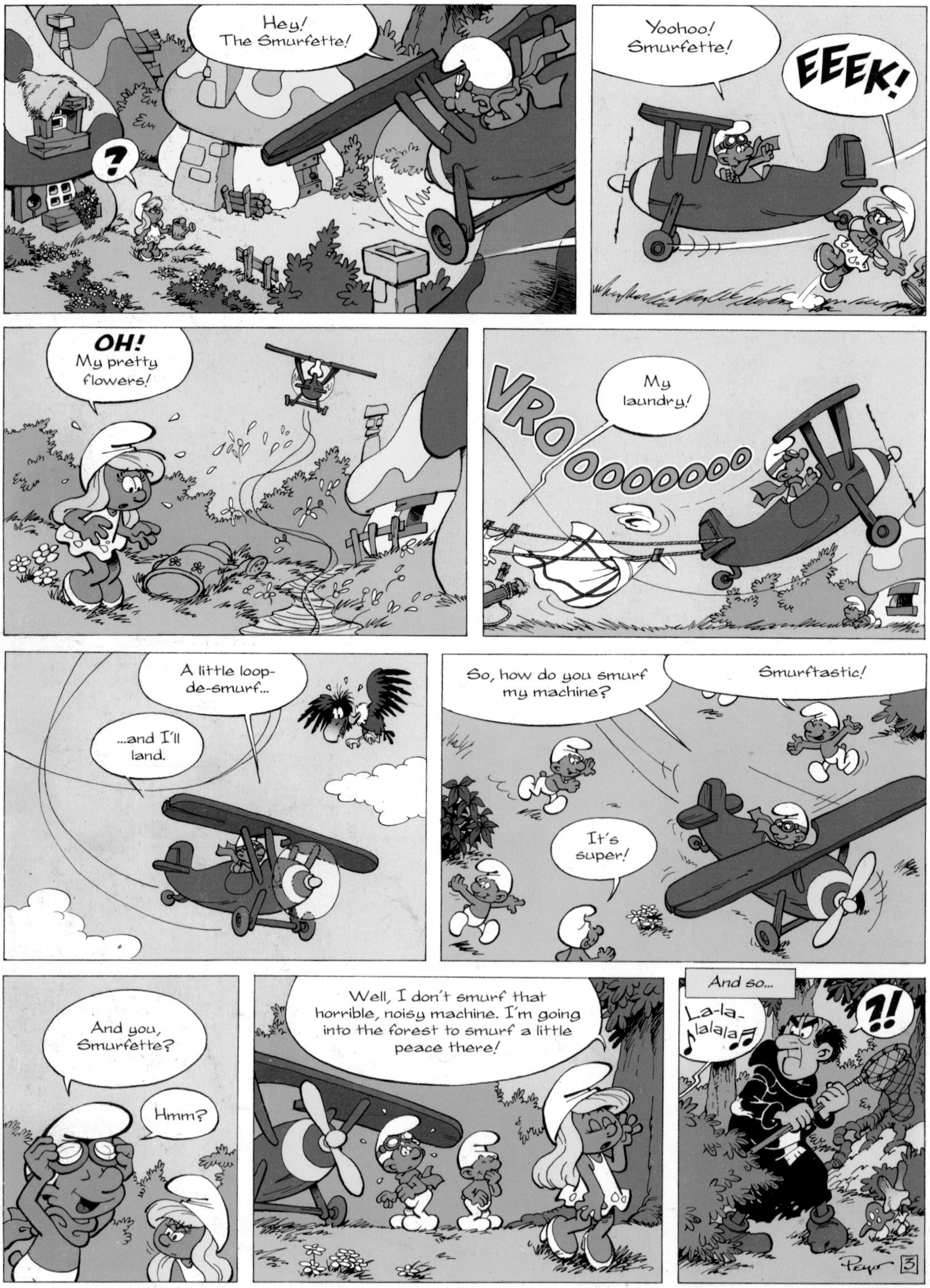

Hey! The Smurfette!
?
Yoohoo! Smurfette!
EEEK!
OH! My pretty flowers!
VROOOOOOOOO
My laundry!
A little loop-de-smurf...
...and I'll land.
So, how do you smurf my machine?
Smurftastic!
It's super!
And you, Smurfette?
Hmm?
Well, I don't smurf that horrible, noisy machine. I'm going into the forest to smurf a little peace there!
And so...
La-la-lalala
?!
Peyo
3

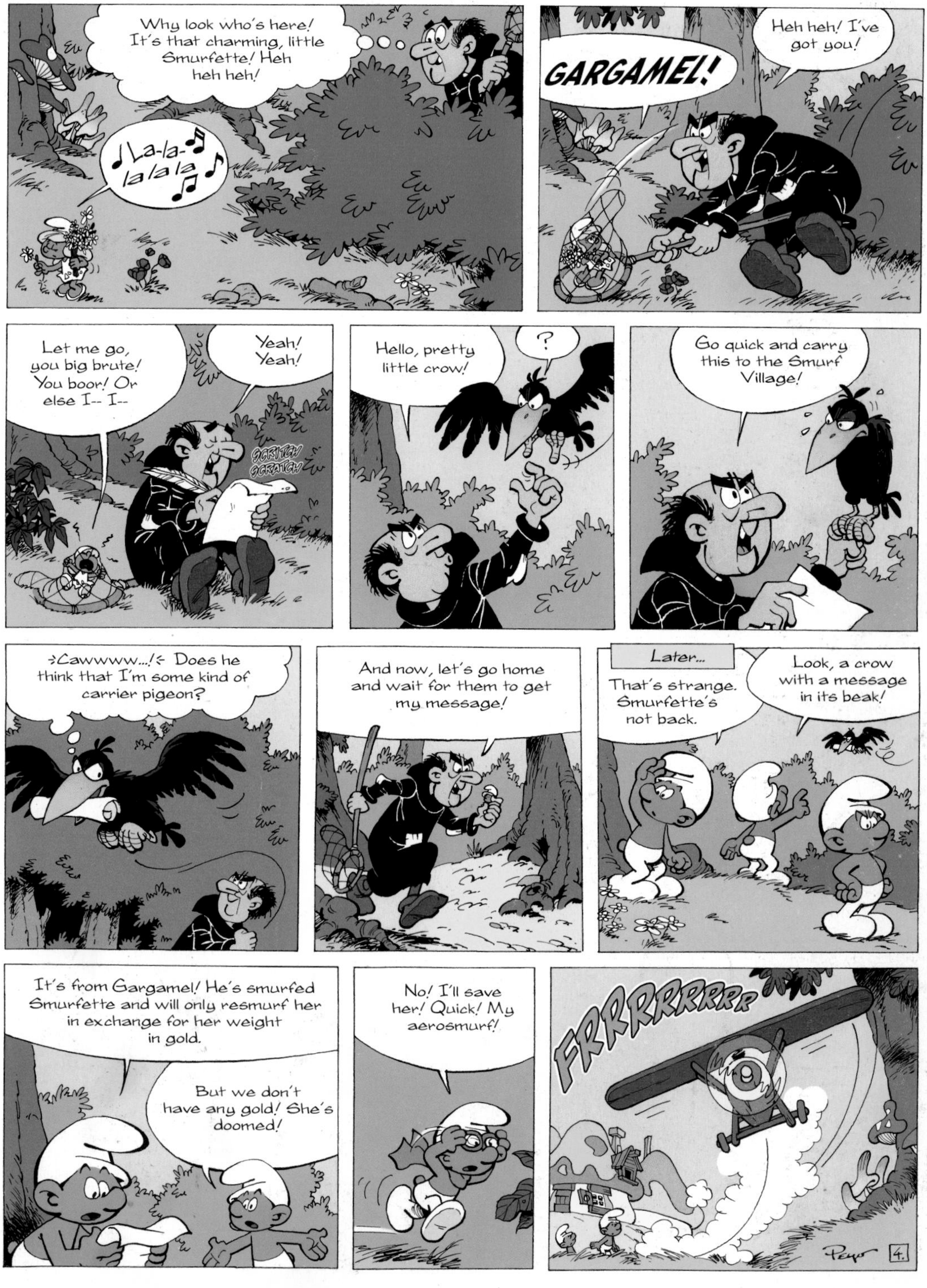

Why look who's here! It's that charming, little Smurfette! Heh heh heh!
La-la-la/a/a
GARGAMEL!
Heh heh! I've got you!
Let me go, you big brute! You boor! Or else I-- I--
Yeah! Yeah!
SCRITCH SCRATCH
Hello, pretty little crow!
?
Go quick and carry this to the Smurf Village!
Cawwww...! Does he think that I'm some kind of carrier pigeon?
And now, let's go home and wait for them to get my message!
Later...
That's strange. Smurfette's not back.
Look, a crow with a message in its beak!
It's from Gargamel! He's smurfed Smurfette and will only resmurf her in exchange for her weight in gold.
But we don't have any gold! She's doomed!
No! I'll save her! Quick! My aerosmurf!
FRRRRRRRR
Peyo
4.

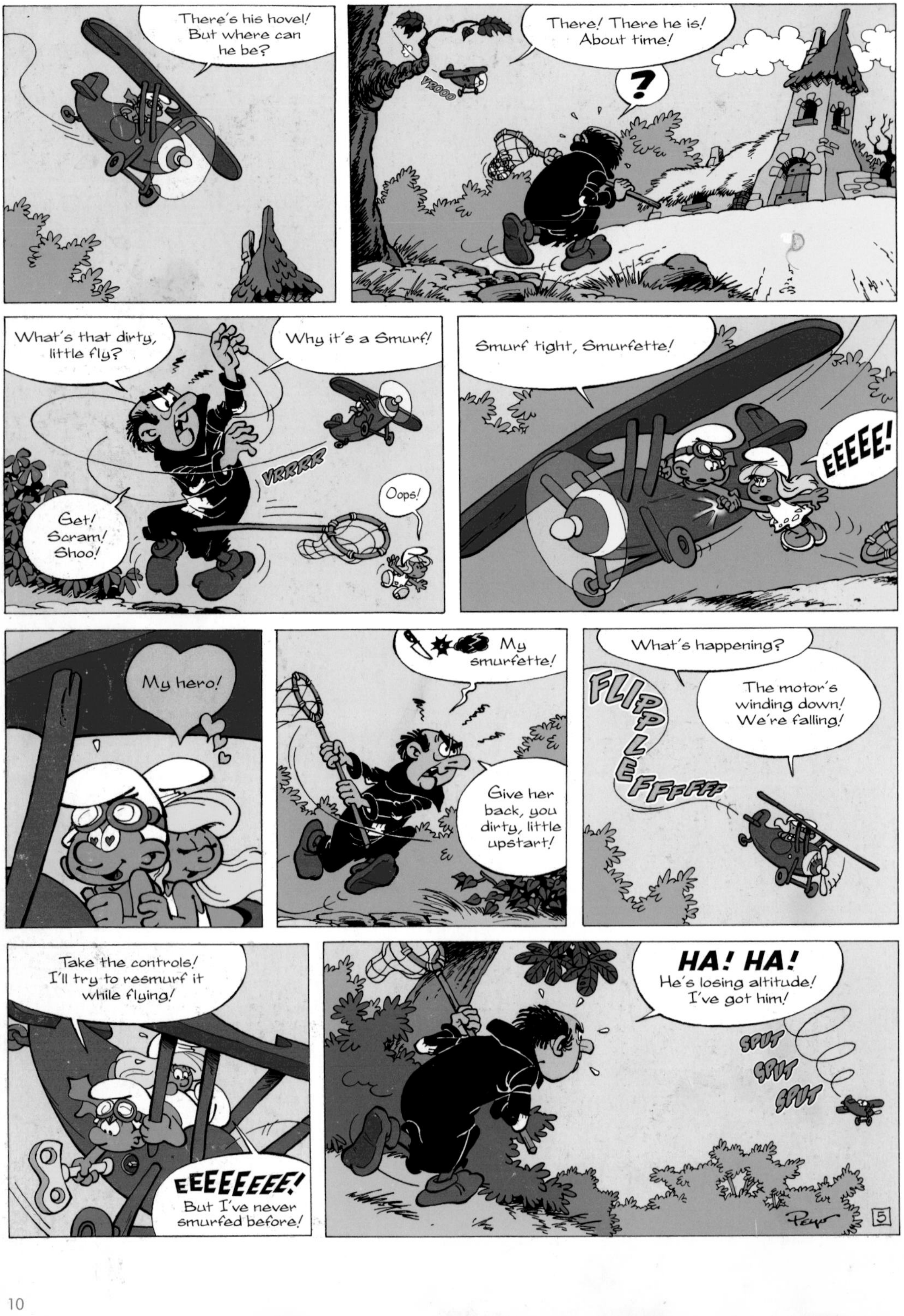
There's his hovel! But where can he be?
VROOO
There! There he is! About time!
?
What's that dirty, little fly?
Why it's a Smurf!
VRRRR
Get! Scram! Shoo!
Oops!
Smurf tight, Smurfette!
EEEEE!
My hero!
My smurfette!
Give her back, you dirty, little upstart!
What's happening?
FLIPPLE
FFFFFF
The motor's winding down! We're falling!
Take the controls! I'll try to resmurf it while flying!
EEEEEEEE! But I've never smurfed before!
HA! HA! He's losing altitude! I've got him!
SPUT
SPUT
SPUT
Peyo
5

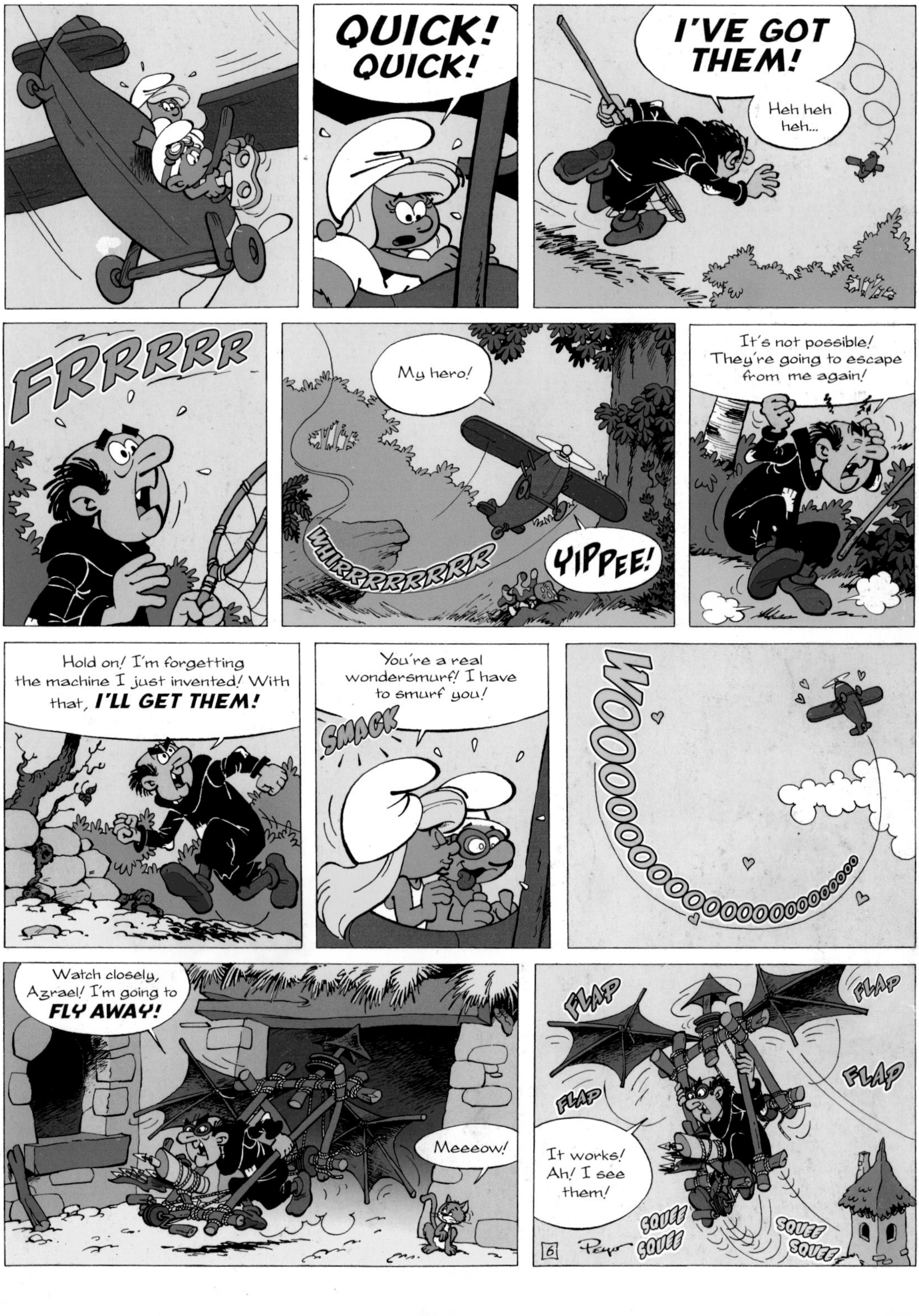
QUICK! QUICK!
I'VE GOT THEM!
Heh heh heh...
FRRRRR
My hero!
WHIRRRRRRRRR
YIPPEE!
It's not possible! They're going to escape from me again!
Hold on! I'm forgetting the machine I just invented! With that, I'LL GET THEM!
You're a real wondersmurf! I have to smurf you!
SMACK
WOOOOOOOOOOOOOOOOOOOOOOOOOOOOOO
Watch closely, Azrael! I'm going to FLY AWAY!
Meeeow!
FLAP
FLAP
FLAP
FLAP
It works! Ah! I see them!
SQUEE SQUEE
SQUEE SQUEE
6
Peyo

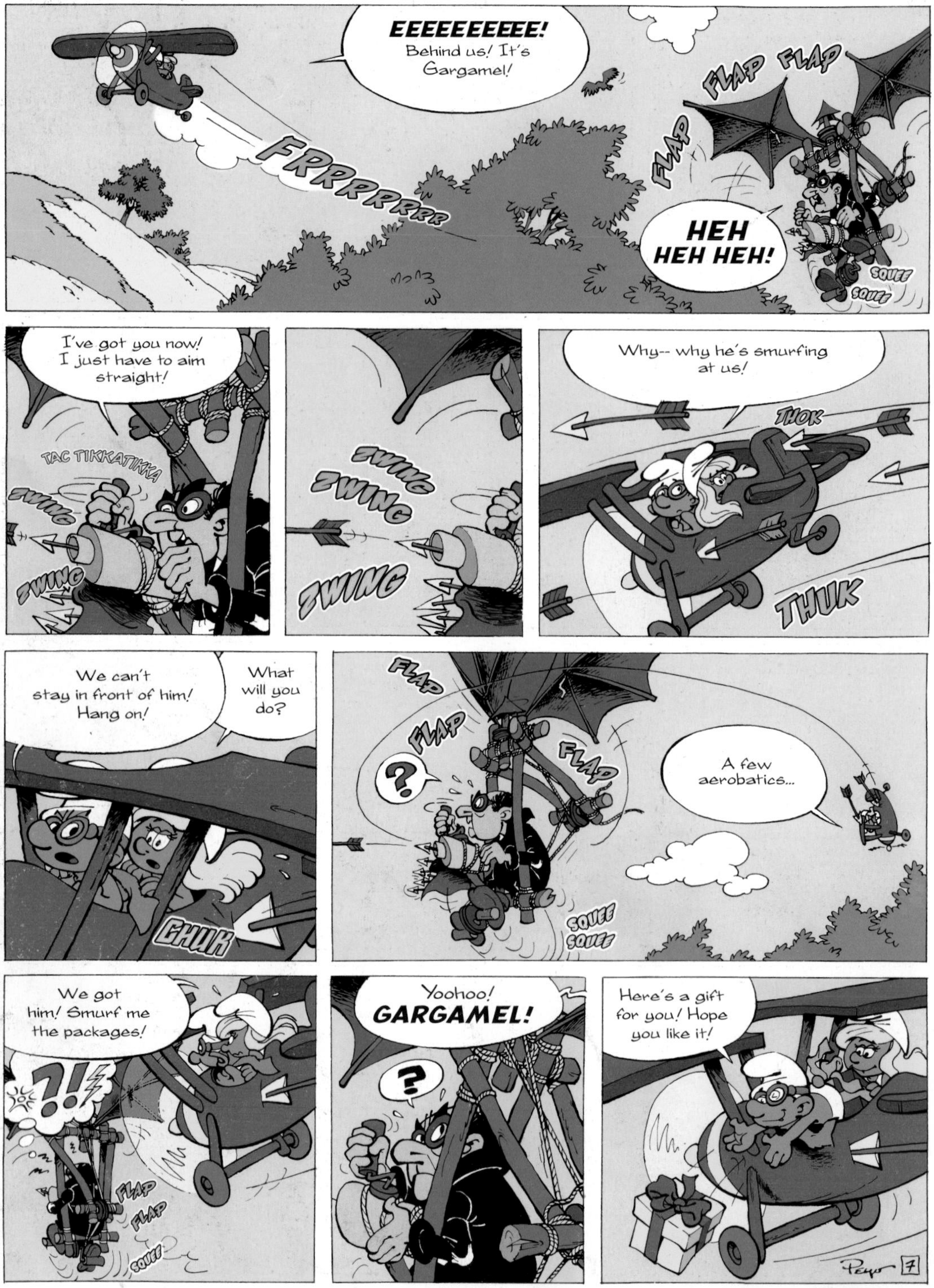
EEEEEEEEEE! Behind us! It's Gargamel!
FRRRRRRRRR
FLAP FLAP FLAP FLAP
HEH HEH HEH!
SQUEE SQUEE
I've got you now! I just have to aim straight!
TAC TIKKATIKKA
ZWING
ZWING
ZWING ZWING
ZWING
Why-- why he's smurfing at us!
THOK
THUK
We can't stay in front of him! Hang on!
What will you do?
GHUK
FLAP
FLAP
FLAP
?
A few aerobatics...
SQUEE SQUEE
We got him! Smurf me the packages!
?!
FLAP FLAP
SQUEE
Yoohoo! GARGAMEL!
?
Here's a gift for you! Hope you like it!
Peyo 7

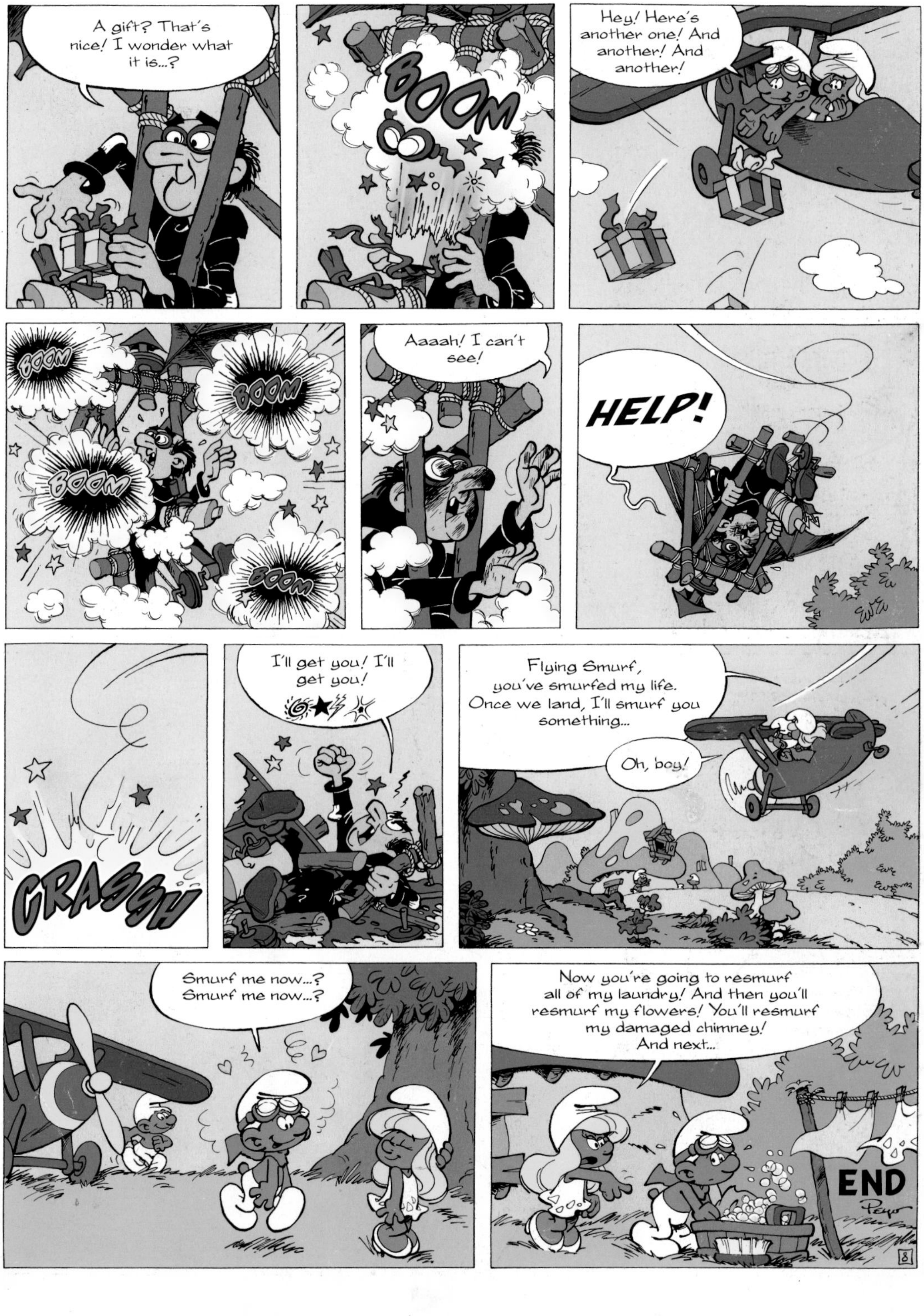
A gift? That's nice! I wonder what it is...?
BOOM
Hey! Here's another one! And another! And another!
BOOM
BOOM
BOOM
BOOM
Aaaah! I can't see!
HELP!
CRASSH
I'll get you! I'll get you!
Flying Smurf, you've smurfed my life. Once we land, I'll smurf you something...
Oh, boy!
Smurf me now...? Smurf me now...?
Now you're going to resmurf all of my laundry! And then you'll resmurf my flowers! You'll resmurf my damaged chimney! And next...
END
Peyo
8

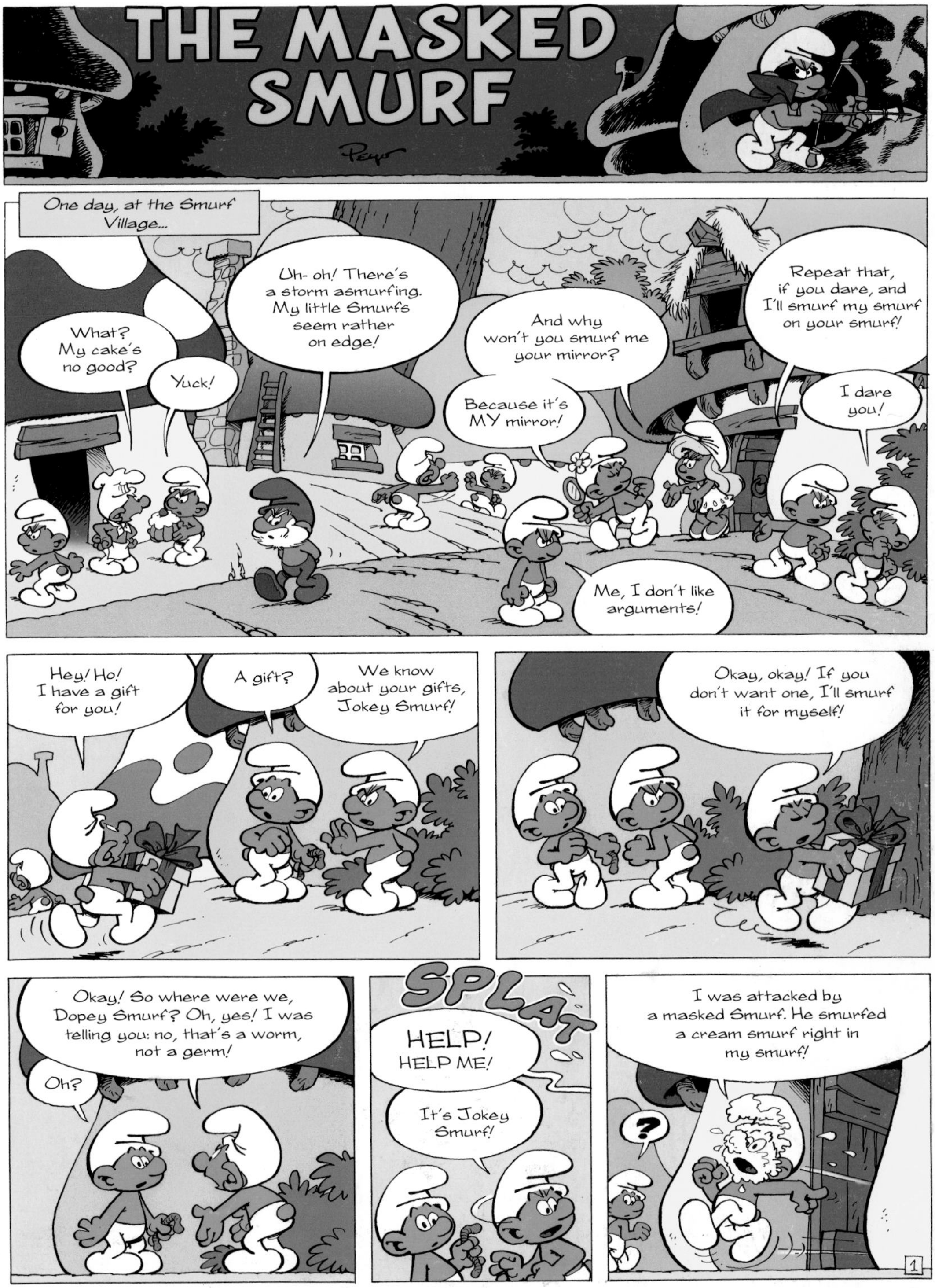
THE MASKED SMURF
Peyo
One day, at the Smurf Village...
What? My cake's no good?
Yuck!
Uh- oh! There's a storm asmurfing. My little Smurfs seem rather on edge!
And why won't you smurf me your mirror?
Because it's MY mirror!
Repeat that, if you dare, and I'll smurf my smurf on your smurf!
I dare you!
Me, I don't like arguments!
Hey! Ho! I have a gift for you!
A gift?
We know about your gifts, Jokey Smurf!
Okay, okay! If you don't want one, I'll smurf it for myself!
Okay! So where were we, Dopey Smurf? Oh, yes! I was telling you: no, that's a worm, not a germ!
Oh?
SPLAT
HELP! HELP ME!
It's Jokey Smurf!
I was attacked by a masked Smurf. He smurfed a cream smurf right in my smurf!
?
1

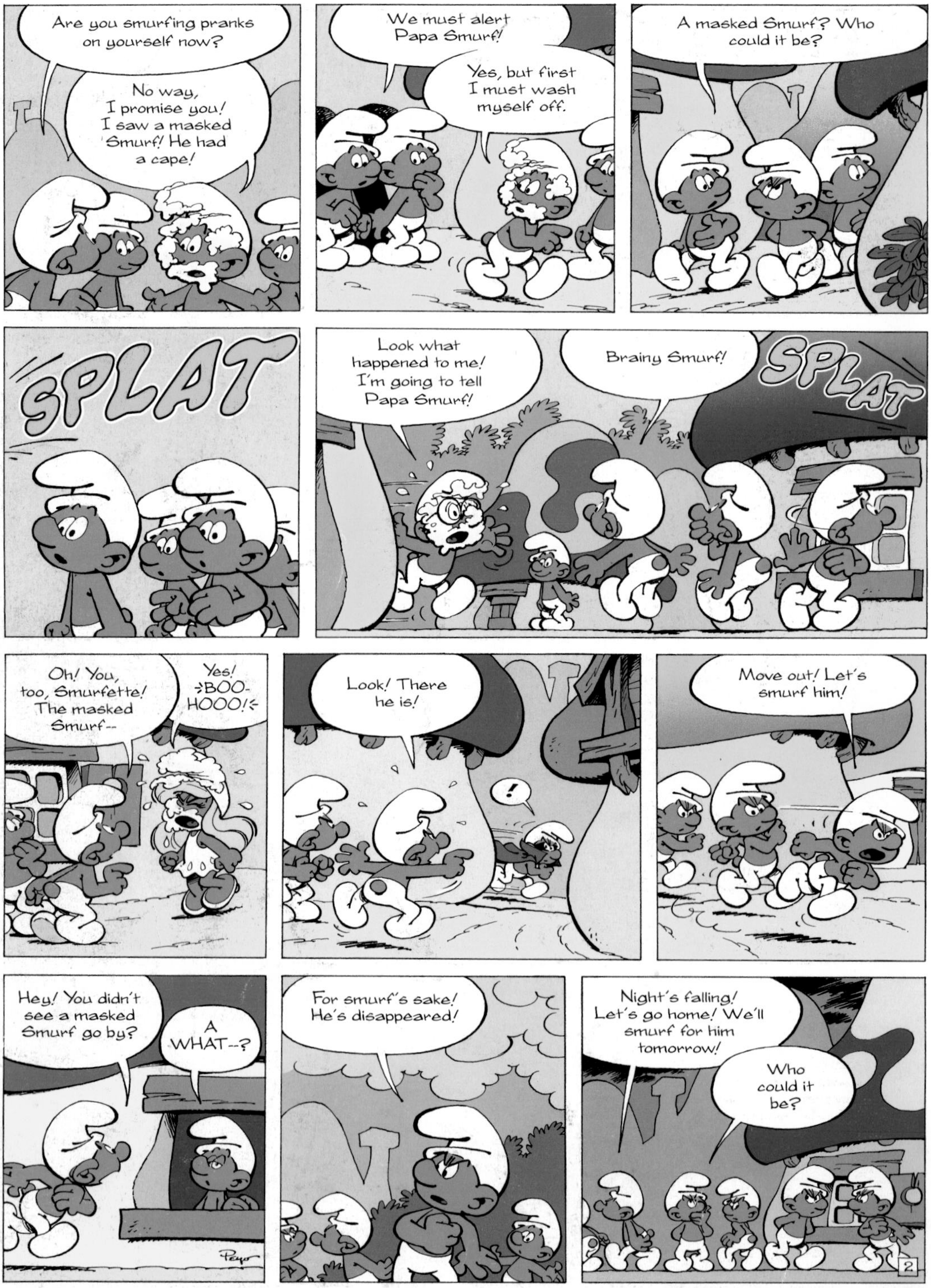
Are you smurfing pranks on yourself now?
No way, I promise you! I saw a masked Smurf! He had a cape!
We must alert Papa Smurf!
Yes, but first I must wash myself off.
A masked Smurf? Who could it be?
SPLAT
Look what happened to me! I'm going to tell Papa Smurf!
Brainy Smurf!
SPLAT
Oh! You, too, Smurfette! The masked Smurf--
Yes! BOO-HOOO!
Look! There he is!
!
Move out! Let's smurf him!
Hey! You didn't see a masked Smurf go by?
A WHAT--?
For smurf's sake! He's disappeared!
Night's falling! Let's go home! We'll smurf for him tomorrow!
Who could it be?
Peyo
2

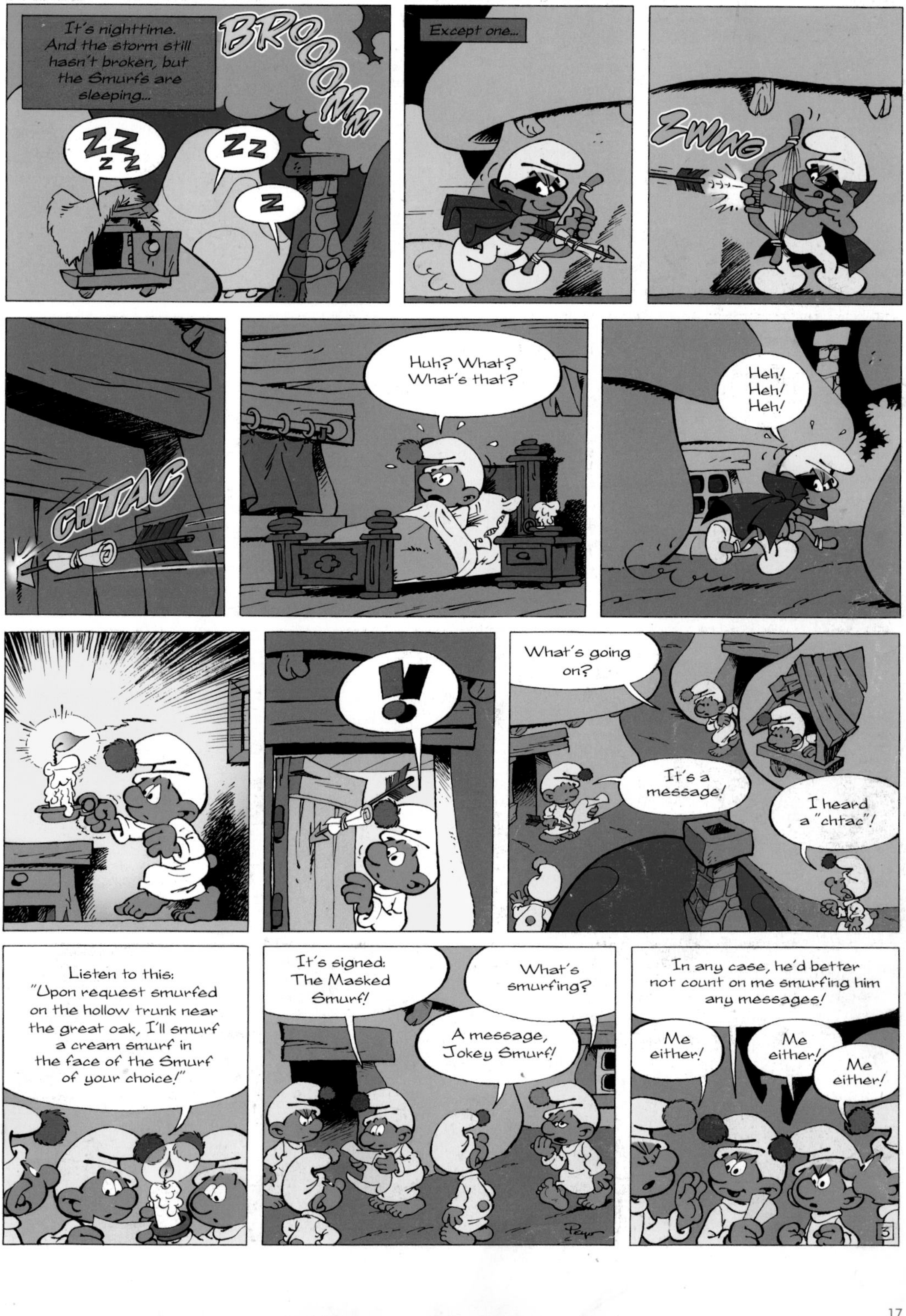
It's nighttime. And the storm still hasn't broken, but the Smurfs are sleeping...
BROOOMM
ZZZ
ZZ
Z
Except one...
ZWING
CHTAC
Huh? What? What's that?
Heh! Heh! Heh!
!
What's going on?
It's a message!
I heard a "chtac"!
Listen to this: "Upon request smurfed on the hollow trunk near the great oak, I'll smurf a cream smurf in the face of the Smurf of your choice!"
It's signed: The Masked Smurf!
What's smurfing?
A message, Jokey Smurf!
In any case, he'd better not count on me smurfing him any messages!
Me either!
Me either!
Me either!
3

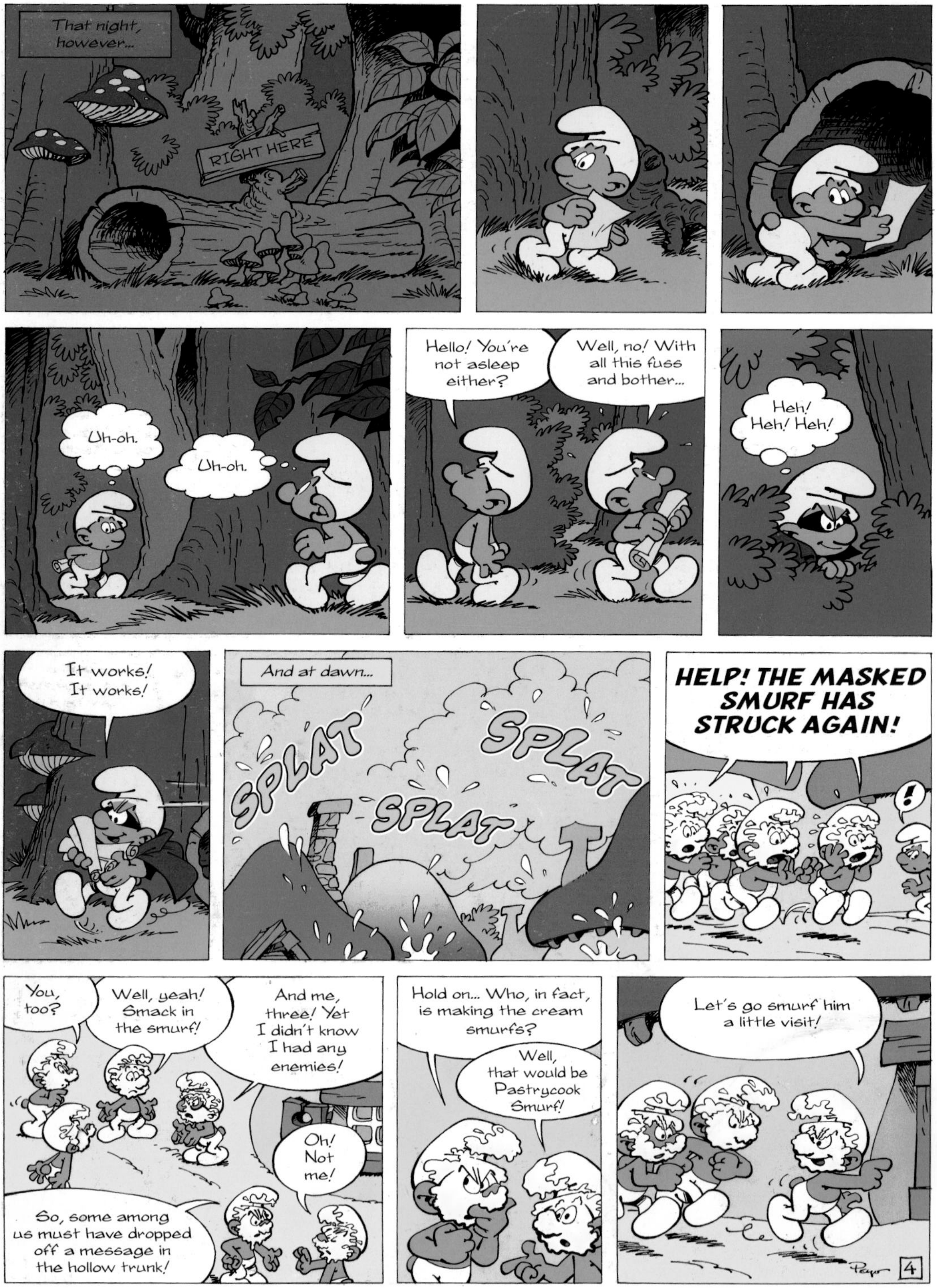
That night, however...
RIGHT HERE
Uh-oh.
Uh-oh.
Hello! You're not asleep either?
Well, no! With all this fuss and bother...
Heh! Heh! Heh!
It works! It works!
And at dawn...
SPLAT
SPLAT
SPLAT
HELP! THE MASKED SMURF HAS STRUCK AGAIN!
!
You, too?
Well, yeah! Smack in the smurf!
And me, three! Yet I didn't know I had any enemies!
Oh! Not me!
So, some among us must have dropped off a message in the hollow trunk!
Hold on... Who, in fact, is making the cream smurfs?
Well, that would be Pastrycook Smurf!
Let's go smurf him a little visit!
Peyo
4

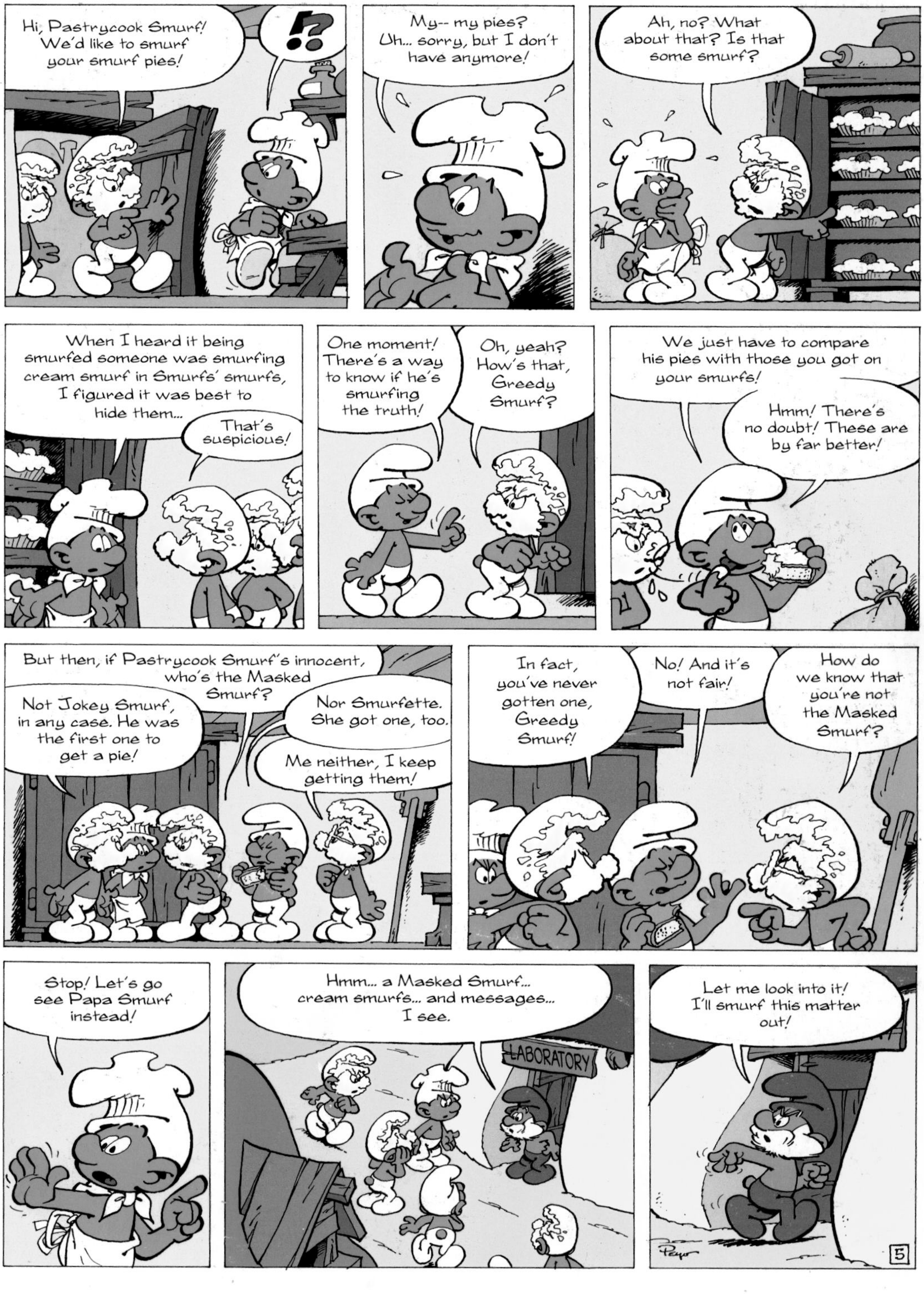
Hi, Pastrycook Smurf! We'd like to smurf your smurf pies!
!?
My-- my pies? Uh... sorry, but I don't have anymore!
Ah, no? What about that? Is that some smurf?
When I heard it being smurfed someone was smurfing cream smurf in Smurfs' smurfs, I figured it was best to hide them...
That's suspicious!
One moment! There's a way to know if he's smurfing the truth!
Oh, yeah? How's that, Greedy Smurf?
We just have to compare his pies with those you got on your smurfs!
Hmm! There's no doubt! These are by far better!
But then, if Pastrycook Smurf's innocent, who's the Masked Smurf?
Not Jokey Smurf, in any case. He was the first one to get a pie!
Nor Smurfette. She got one, too.
Me neither, I keep getting them!
In fact, you've never gotten one, Greedy Smurf!
No! And it's not fair!
How do we know that you're not the Masked Smurf?
Stop! Let's go see Papa Smurf instead!
Hmm... a Masked Smurf... cream smurfs... and messages... I see.
LABORATORY
Let me look into it! I'll smurf this matter out!
5

I have an idea! I'm going to smurf him a message!

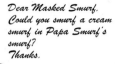 
Dear Masked Smurf,
Could you smurf a cream smurf in Papa Smurf's smurf?
Thanks.

And I'll smurf indelible white ink on the back of the sheet.

It's done!

Now I just have to wait!

And that night...
I wonder if anyone's smurfed me any more messages...

Ho, ho! There's lots of work for a Masked Smurf!

I'll have to smurf some new pies! Heh! Heh! Heh!

The next day at dawn...

SPLAT SPLAT
Oh, no!
Enough!

Hee! Hee! Hee!

6

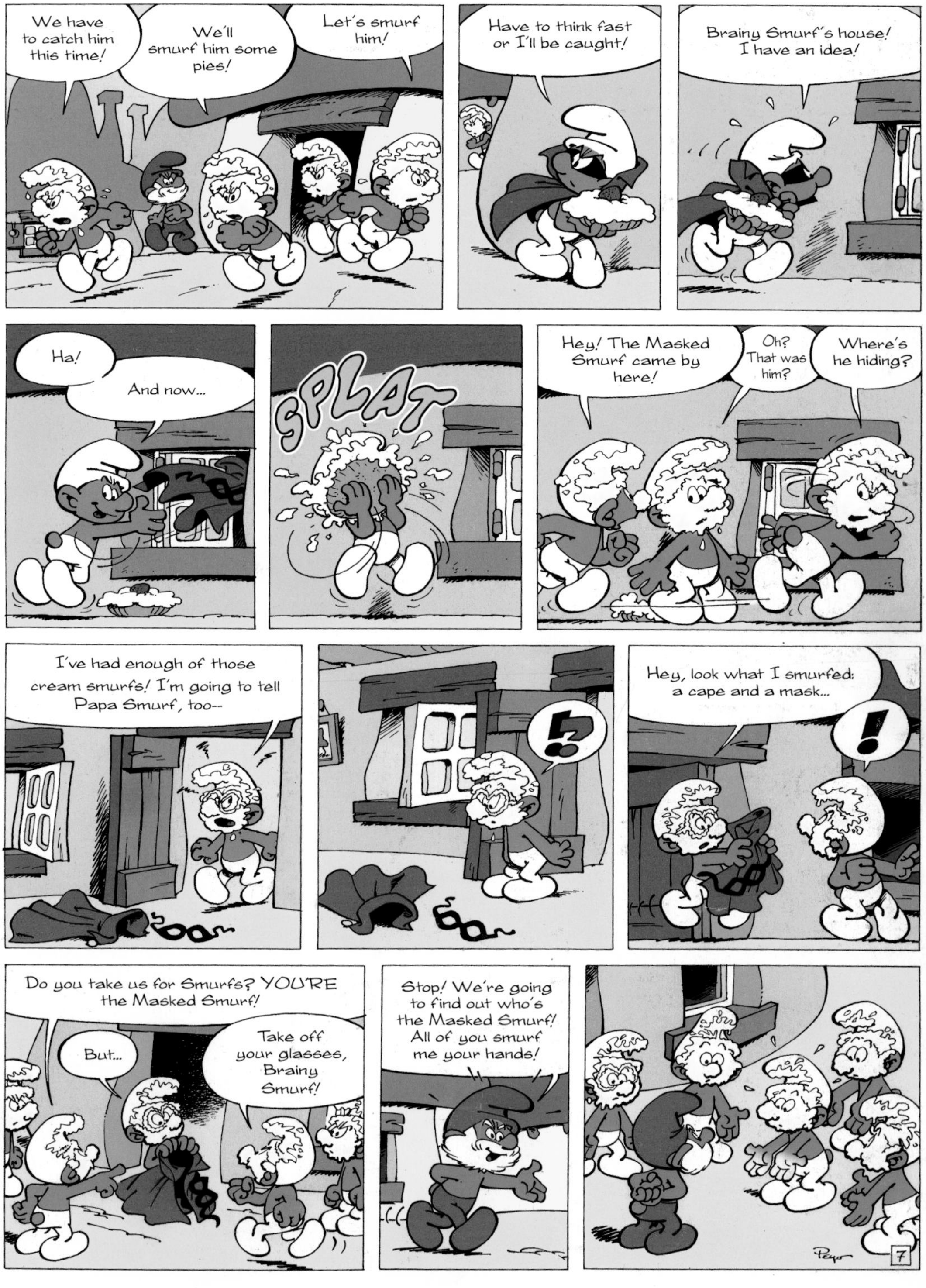
We have to catch him this time!
We'll smurf him some pies!
Let's smurf him!
Have to think fast or I'll be caught!
Brainy Smurf's house! I have an idea!
Ha!
And now...
SPLAT
Hey! The Masked Smurf came by here!
Oh? That was him?
Where's he hiding?
I've had enough of those cream smurfs! I'm going to tell Papa Smurf, too--
?
Hey, look what I smurfed: a cape and a mask...
!
Do you take us for Smurfs? YOU'RE the Masked Smurf!
But...
Take off your glasses, Brainy Smurf!
Stop! We're going to find out who's the Masked Smurf! All of you smurf me your hands!
7

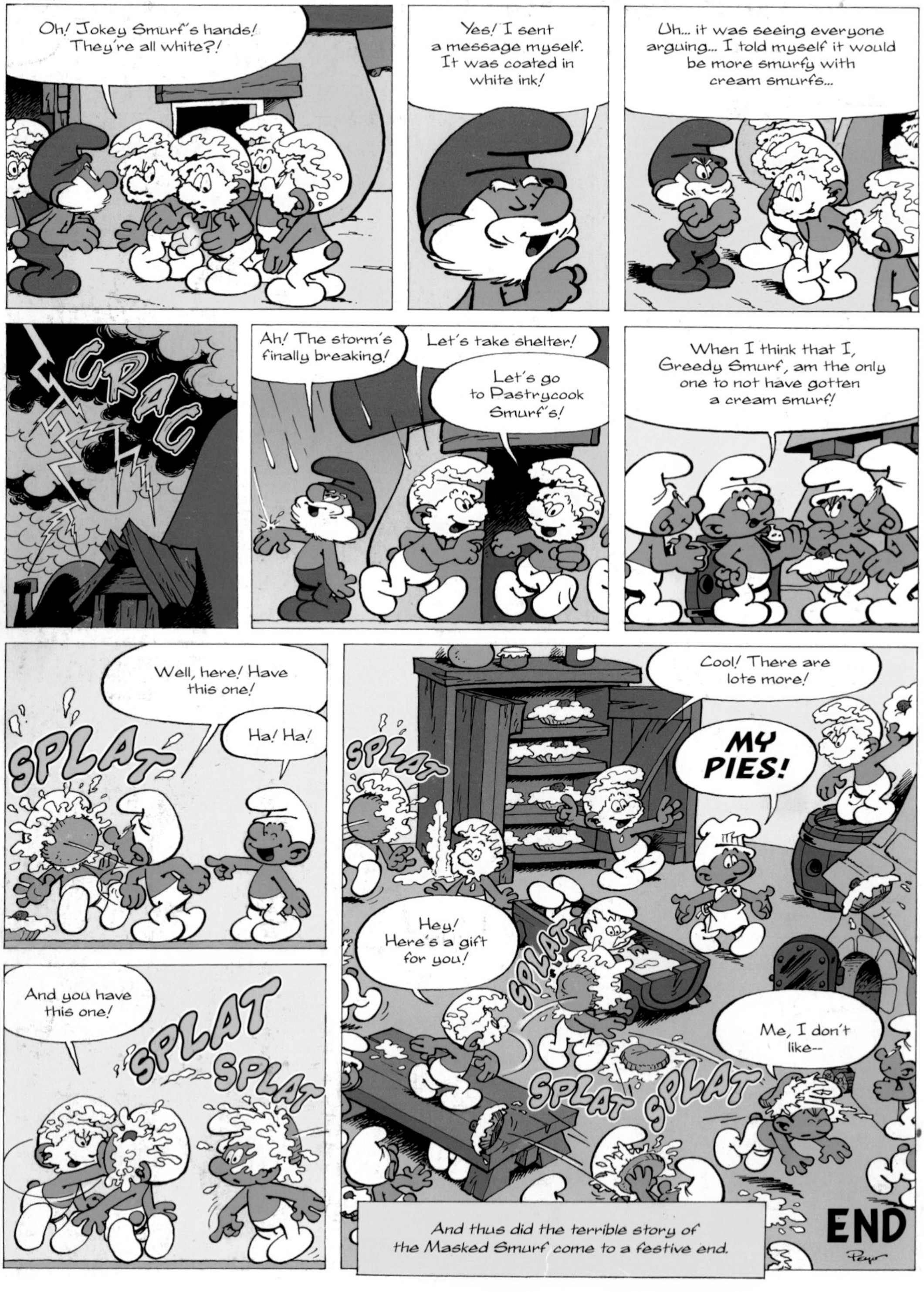
Oh! Jokey Smurf's hands! They're all white?!
Yes! I sent a message myself. It was coated in white ink!
Uh... it was seeing everyone arguing... I told myself it would be more smurfy with cream smurfs...
CRAC
Ah! The storm's finally breaking!
Let's take shelter!
Let's go to Pastrycook Smurf's!
When I think that I, Greedy Smurf, am the only one to not have gotten a cream smurf!
Well, here! Have this one!
Ha! Ha!
SPLAT
Cool! There are lots more!
MY PIES!
SPLAT
Hey! Here's a gift for you!
SPLAT
And you have this one!
SPLAT
SPLAT
SPLAT
SPLAT
Me, I don't like--
And thus did the terrible story of the Masked Smurf come to a festive end.
END
Peyo

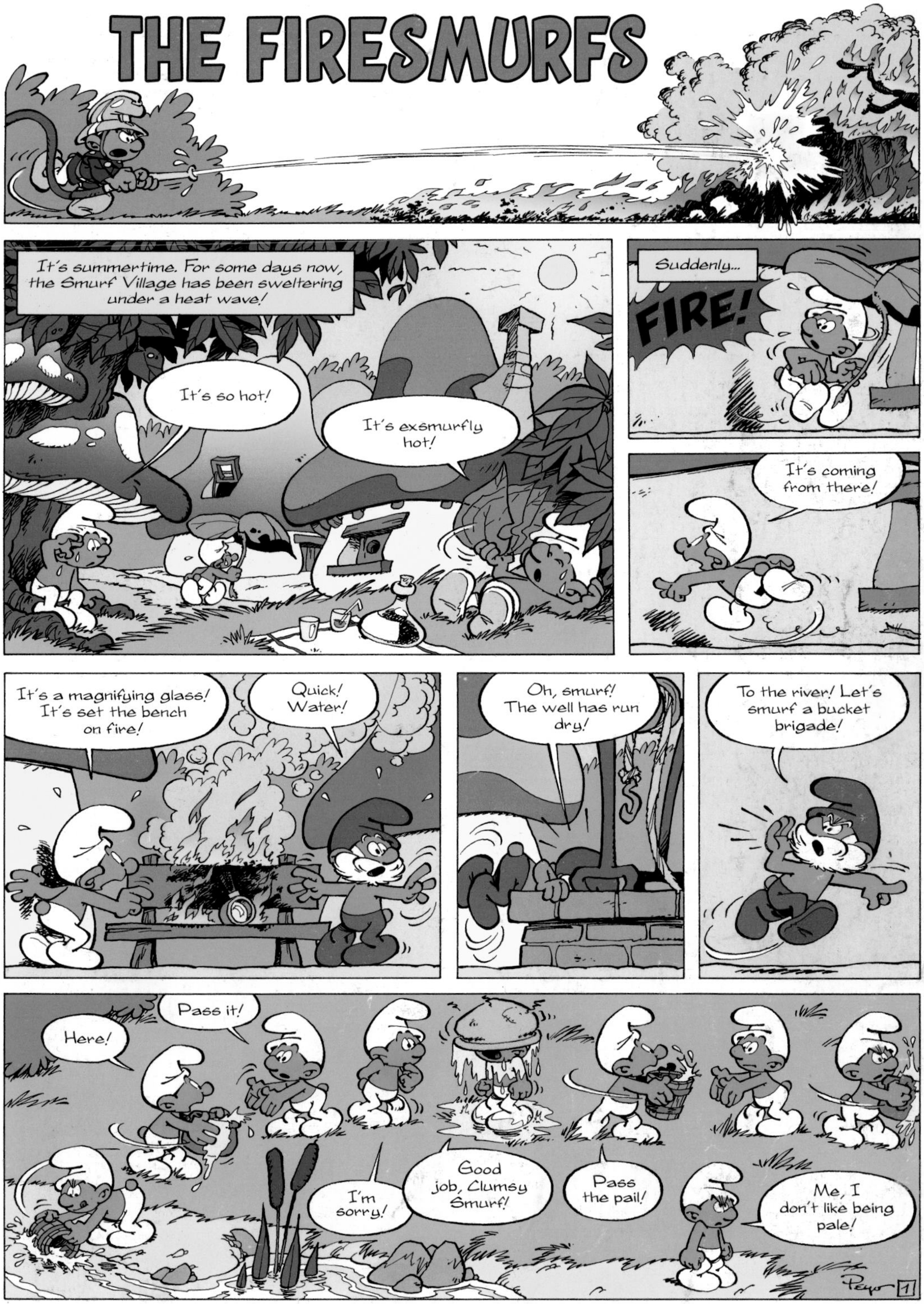
THE FIRESMURFS
It's summertime. For some days now, the Smurf Village has been sweltering under a heat wave!
It's so hot!
It's exsmurfly hot!
Suddenly...
FIRE!
It's coming from there!
It's a magnifying glass! It's set the bench on fire!
Quick! Water!
Oh, smurf! The well has run dry!
To the river! Let's smurf a bucket brigade!
Here!
Pass it!
I'm sorry!
Good job, Clumsy Smurf!
Pass the pail!
Me, I don't like being pale!
Peyo
1

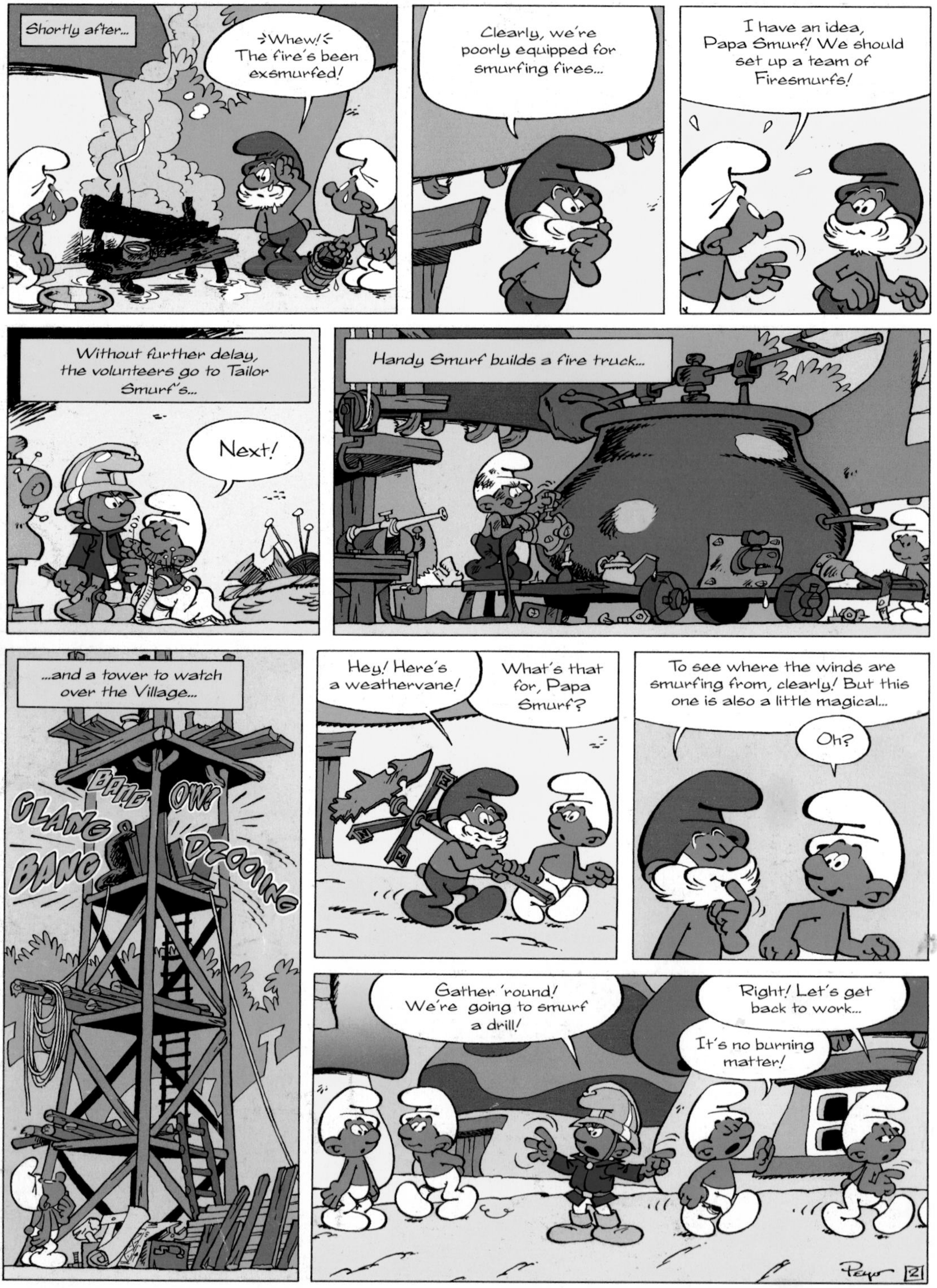
Shortly after...
Whew! The fire's been exsmurfed!
Clearly, we're poorly equipped for smurfing fires...
I have an idea, Papa Smurf! We should set up a team of Firesmurfs!
Without further delay, the volunteers go to Tailor Smurf's...
Next!
Handy Smurf builds a fire truck...
...and a tower to watch over the Village...
BANG
OW!
CLANG
BANG
DZOOING
Hey! Here's a weathervane!
What's that for, Papa Smurf?
To see where the winds are smurfing from, clearly! But this one is also a little magical...
Oh?
Gather 'round! We're going to smurf a drill!
Right! Let's get back to work...
It's no burning matter!
Peyo

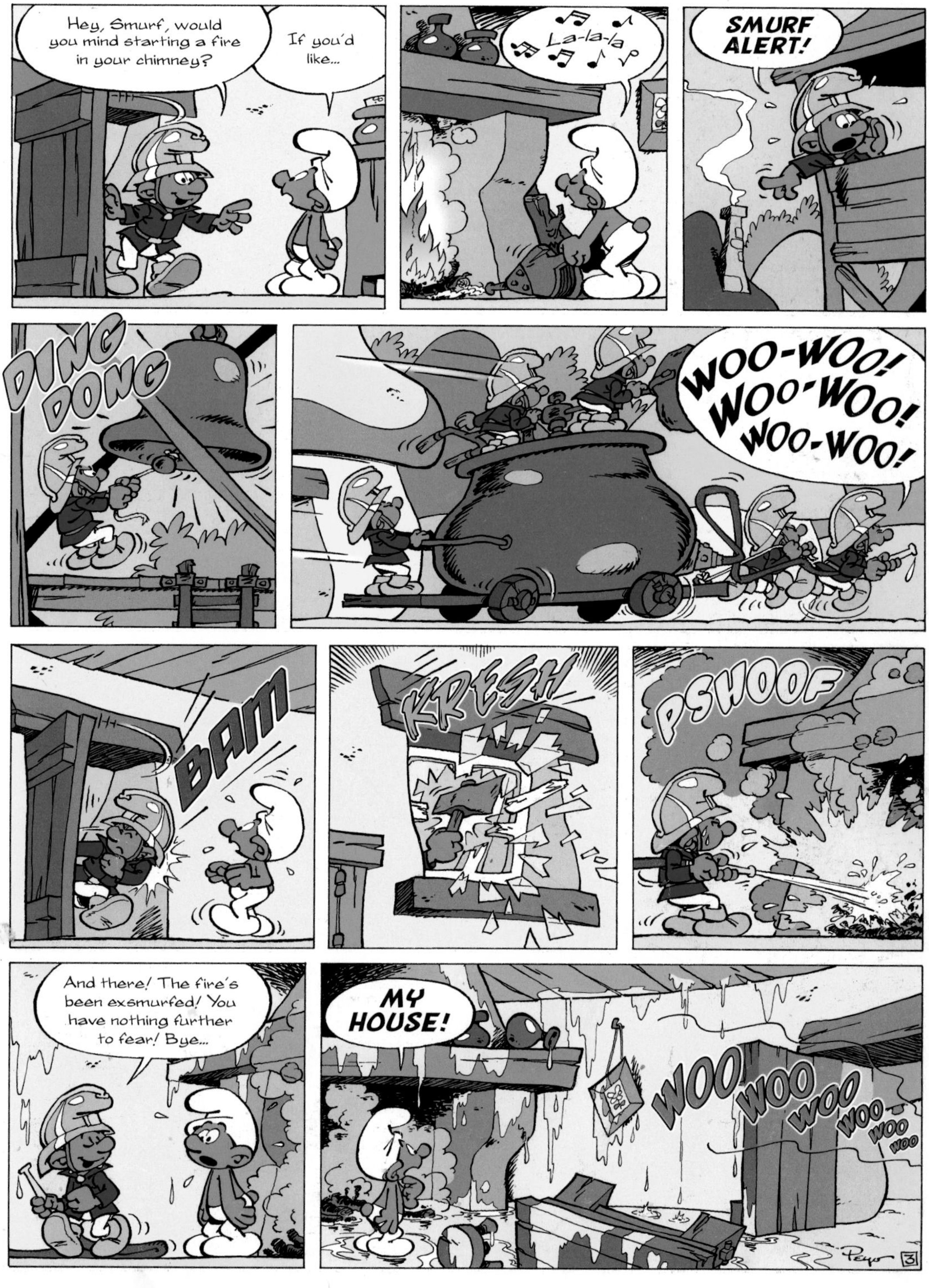
Hey, Smurf, would you mind starting a fire in your chimney?
If you'd like...
La-la-la
SMURF ALERT!
DING DONG
WOO-WOO! WOO-WOO! WOO-WOO!
BAM
KRESH
PSHOOF
And there! The fire's been exsmurfed! You have nothing further to fear! Bye...
MY HOUSE!
WOO WOO WOO WOO WOO WOO
Peyo
3

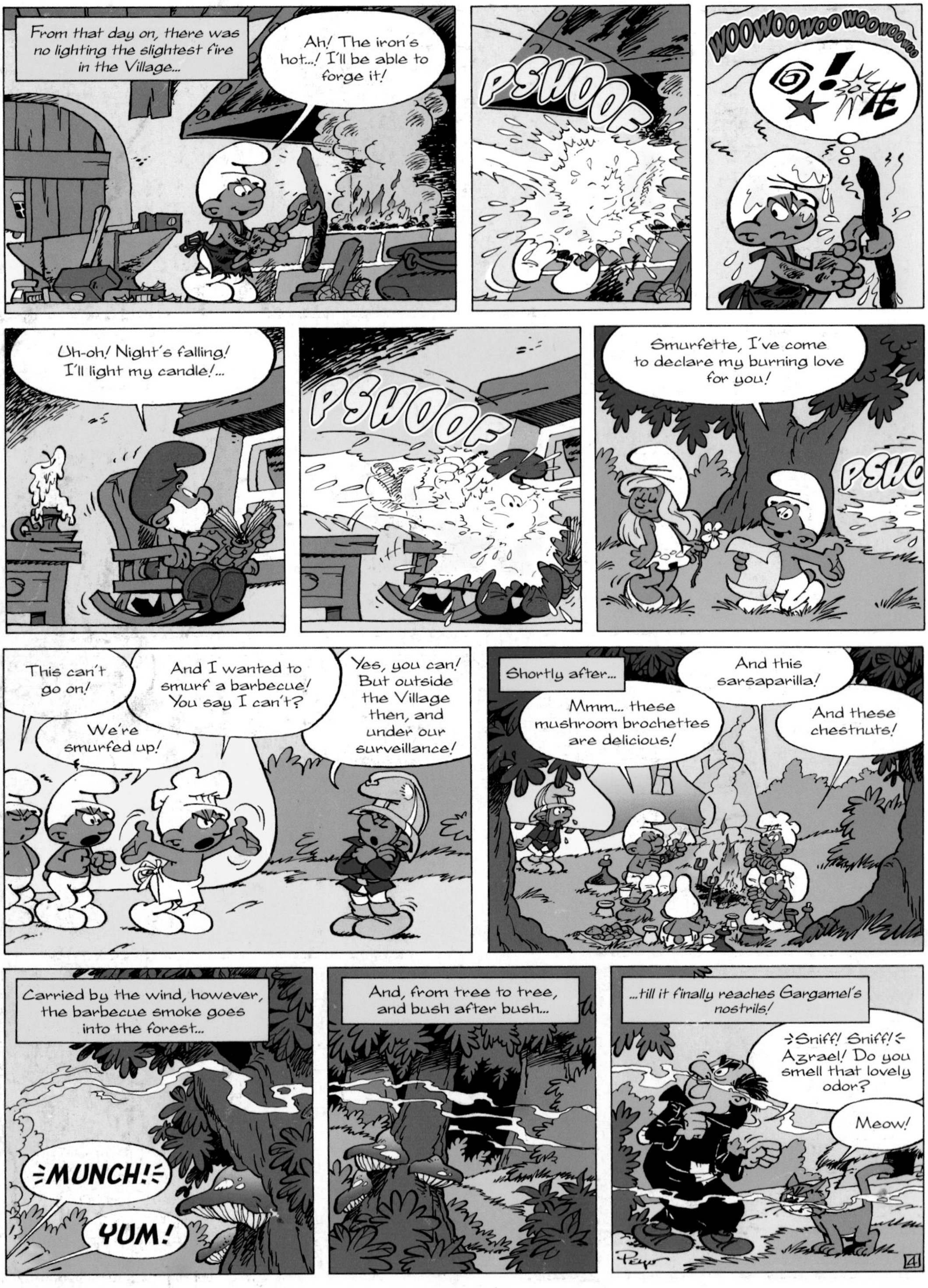
From that day on, there was no lighting the slightest fire in the Village...
Ah! The iron's hot...! I'll be able to forge it!
PSHOOF
WOOWOOWOO WOOWOOWOO
Uh-oh! Night's falling! I'll light my candle!...
PSHOOF
Smurfette, I've come to declare my burning love for you!
PSHO
This can't go on!
We're smurfed up!
And I wanted to smurf a barbecue! You say I can't?
Yes, you can! But outside the Village then, and under our surveillance!
Shortly after...
Mmm... these mushroom brochettes are delicious!
And this sarsaparilla!
And these chestnuts!
Carried by the wind, however, the barbecue smoke goes into the forest...
MUNCH!
YUM!
And, from tree to tree, and bush after bush...
...till it finally reaches Gargamel's nostrils!
Sniff! Sniff! Azrael! Do you smell that lovely odor?
Meow!
Peyo
41

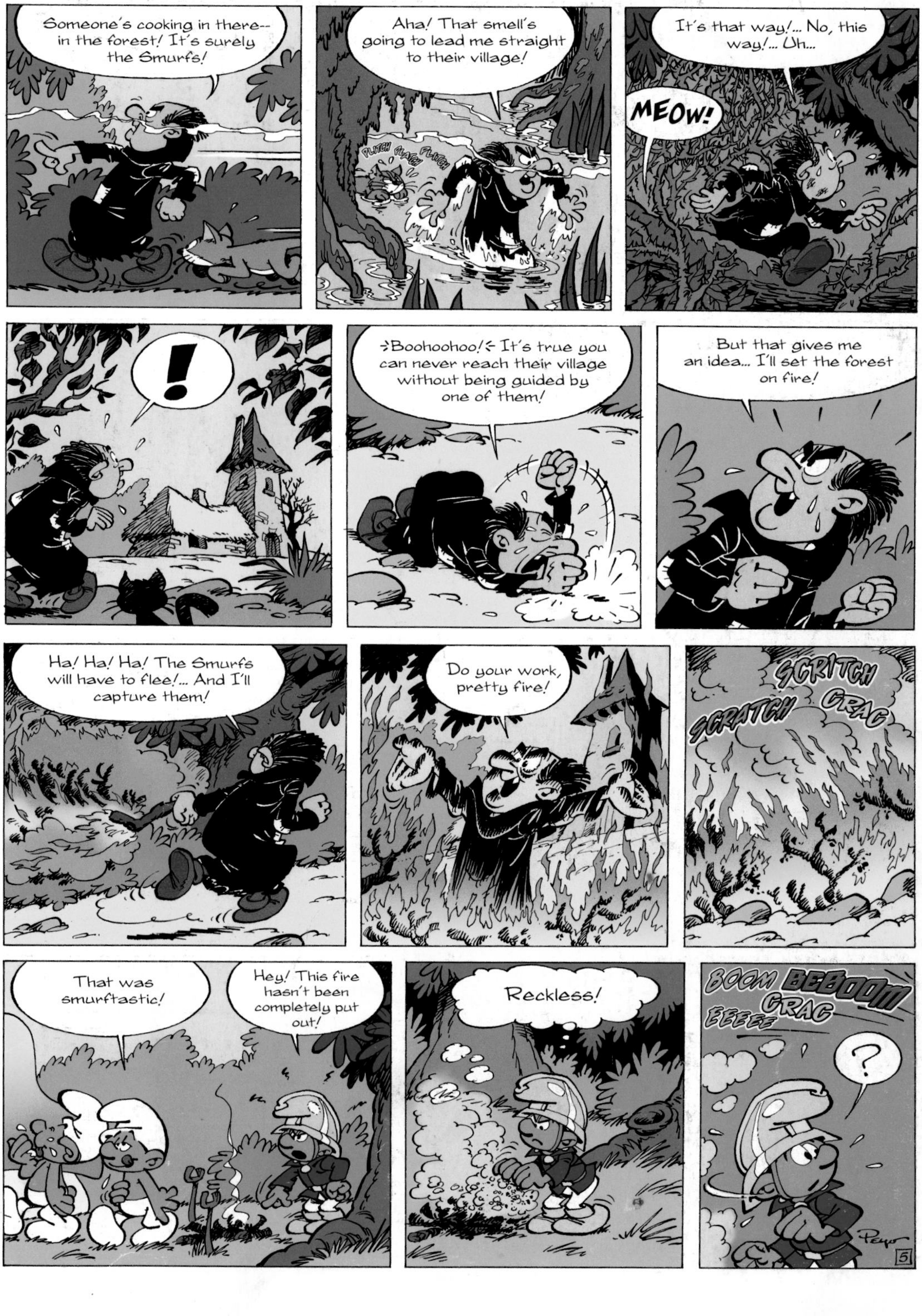
Someone's cooking in there-- in the forest! It's surely the Smurfs!
Aha! That smell's going to lead me straight to their village!
PLITCH PLAGH PLITCH
It's that way!... No, this way!... Uh...
MEOW!
!
Boohoohoo! It's true you can never reach their village without being guided by one of them!
But that gives me an idea... I'll set the forest on fire!
Ha! Ha! Ha! The Smurfs will have to flee!... And I'll capture them!
Do your work, pretty fire!
SCRITCH
SCRATCH
CRAC
That was smurftastic!
Hey! This fire hasn't been completely put out!
Reckless!
BOOM BEBOOM
CRAC
EEEEE
?
Peyo
5

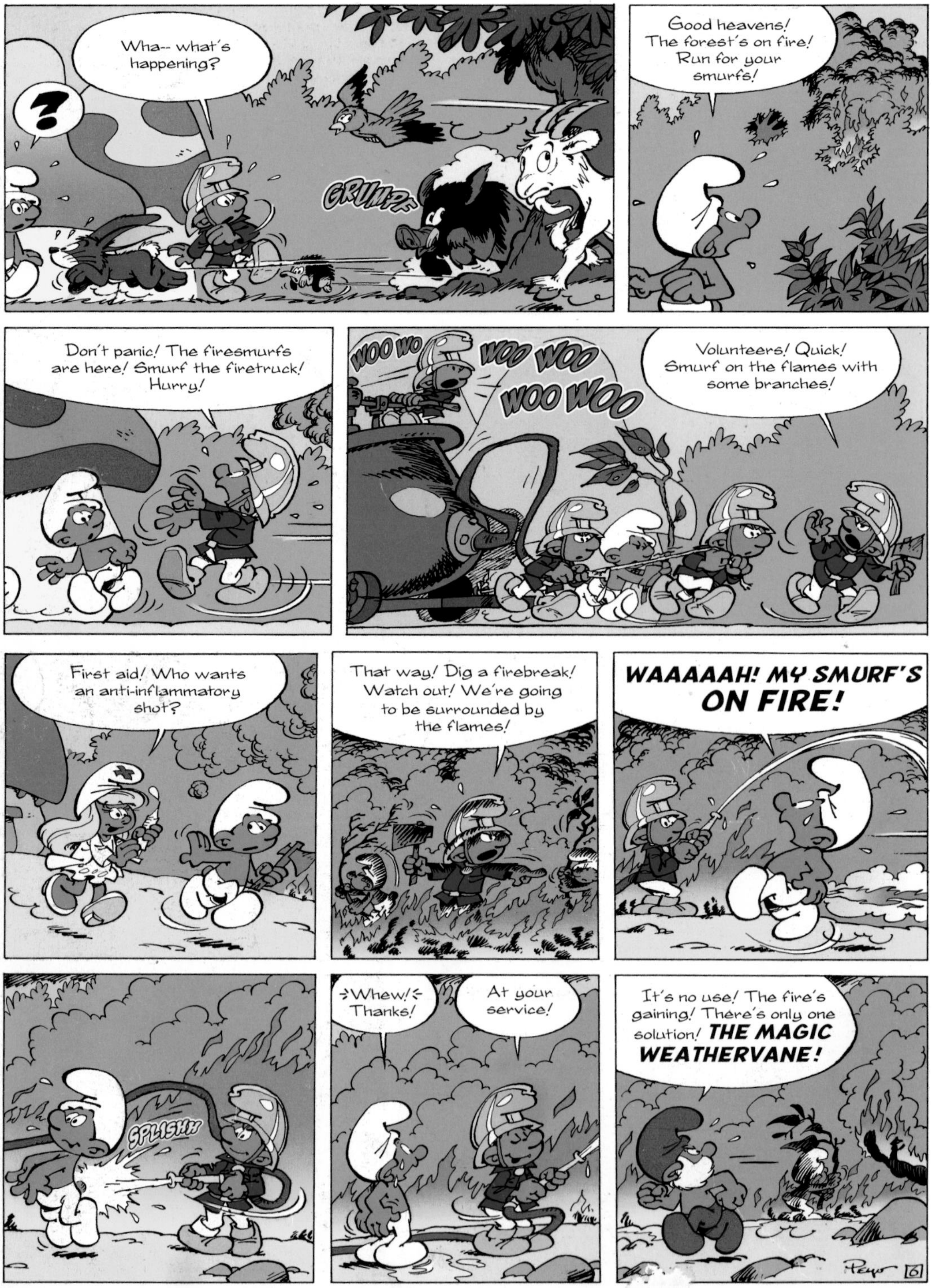

?
Wha-- what's happening?
GRUMPF
Good heavens! The forest's on fire! Run for your smurfs!
Don't panic! The firesmurfs are here! Smurf the firetruck! Hurry!
WOO WO
WOO WOO
WOO WOO
Volunteers! Quick! Smurf on the flames with some branches!
First aid! Who wants an anti-inflammatory shot?
That way! Dig a firebreak! Watch out! We're going to be surrounded by the flames!
WAAAAAH! MY SMURF'S ON FIRE!
SPLISH!!
Whew! Thanks!
At your service!
It's no use! The fire's gaining! There's only one solution! THE MAGIC WEATHERVANE!
Peyo
6

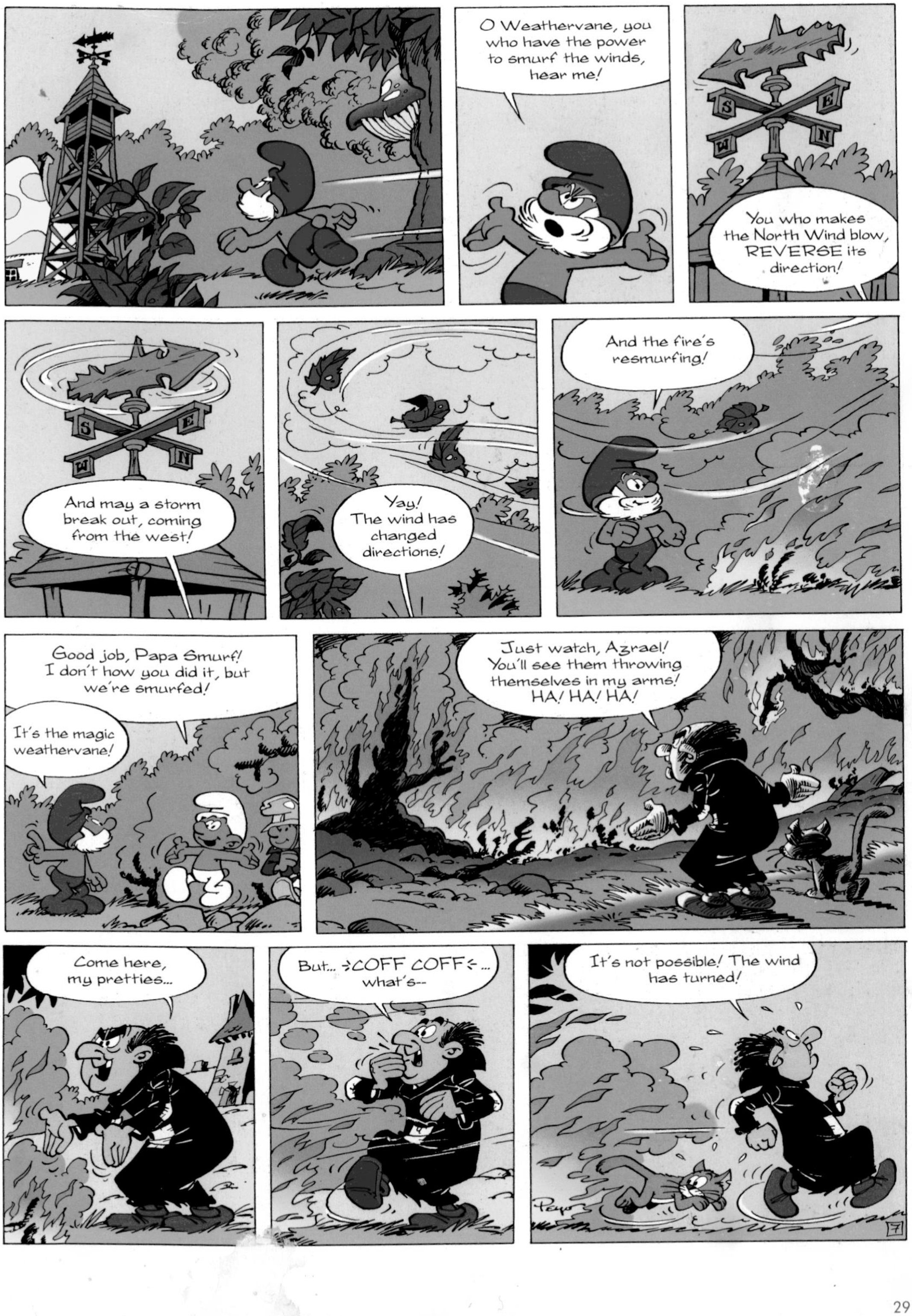
O Weathervane, you who have the power to smurf the winds, hear me!
You who makes the North Wind blow, REVERSE its direction!
And may a storm break out, coming from the west!
Yay! The wind has changed directions!
And the fire's resmurfing!
Good job, Papa Smurf! I don't how you did it, but we're smurfed!
It's the magic weathervane!
Just watch, Azrael! You'll see them throwing themselves in my arms! HA! HA! HA!
Come here, my pretties...
But... COFF COFF ... what's--
It's not possible! The wind has turned!
Peyo
7

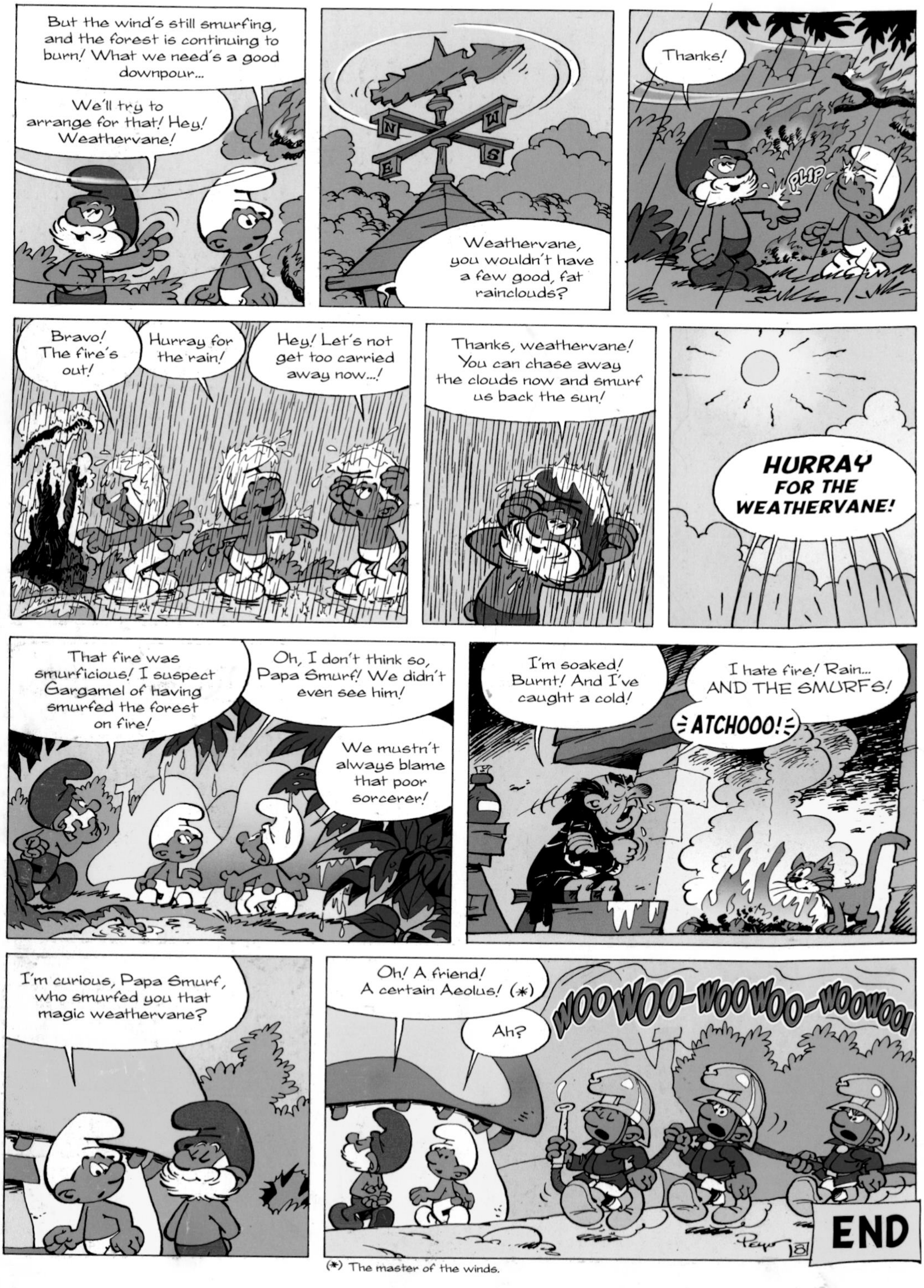
But the wind's still smurfing, and the forest is continuing to burn! What we need's a good downpour...
We'll try to arrange for that! Hey! Weathervane!
N
W
E
S
Weathervane, you wouldn't have a few good, fat rainclouds?
Thanks!
PLIP
Bravo! The fire's out!
Hurray for the rain!
Hey! Let's not get too carried away now...!
Thanks, weathervane! You can chase away the clouds now and smurf us back the sun!
HURRAY FOR THE WEATHERVANE!
That fire was smurficious! I suspect Gargamel of having smurfed the forest on fire!
Oh, I don't think so, Papa Smurf! We didn't even see him!
We mustn't always blame that poor sorcerer!
I'm soaked! Burnt! And I've caught a cold!
I hate fire! Rain... AND THE SMURFS!
ATCHOOO!
I'm curious, Papa Smurf, who smurfed you that magic weathervane?
Oh! A friend! A certain Aeolus! (*)
Ah?
WOOWOO-WOOWOO-WOOWOO!
END

(*) The master of the winds.

GLUTTONY AND THE SMURFS

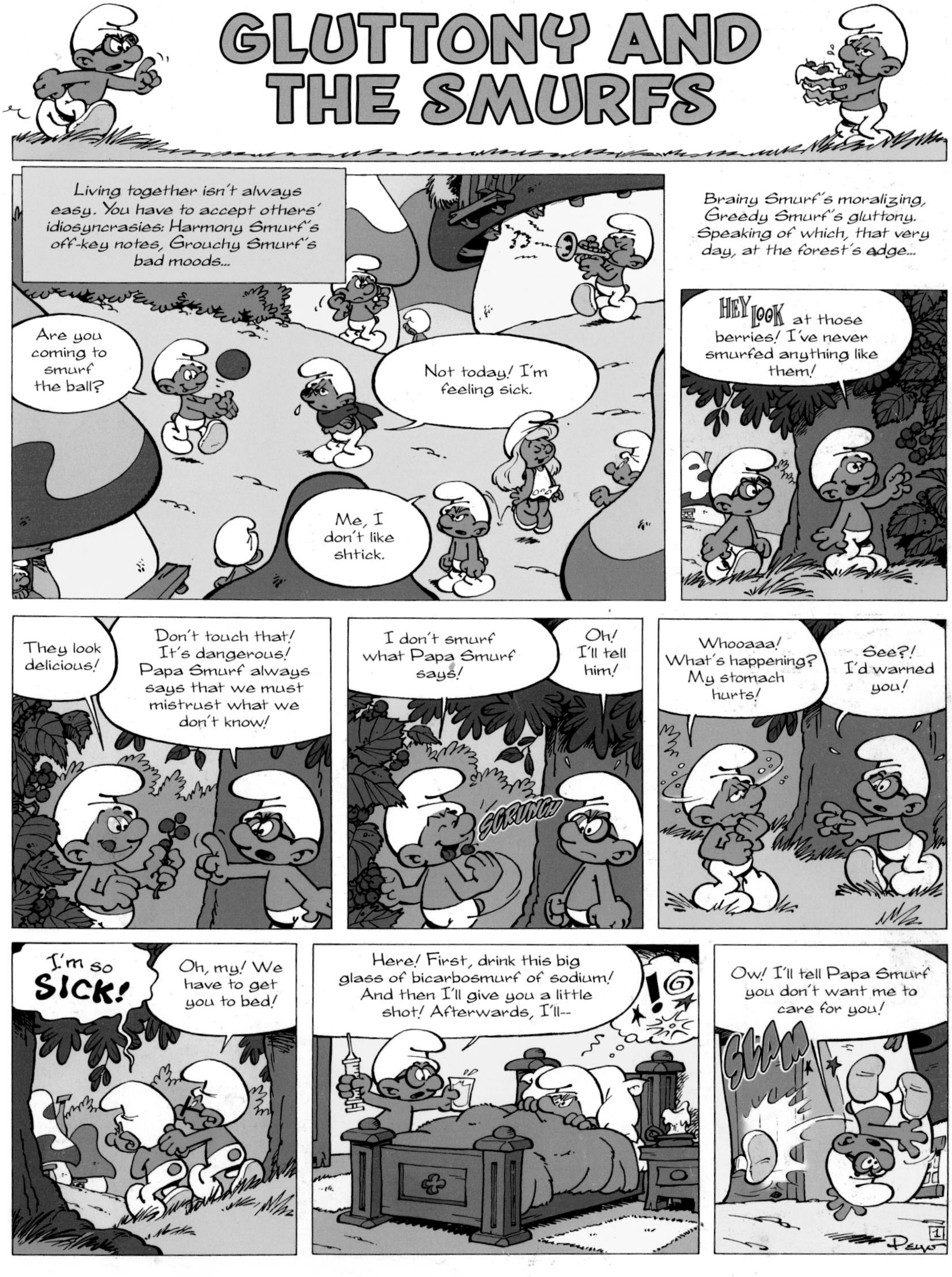
Living together isn't always easy. You have to accept others' idiosyncrasies: Harmony Smurf's off-key notes, Grouchy Smurf's bad moods...
Are you coming to smurf the ball?
Not today! I'm feeling sick.
Me, I don't like shtick.
Brainy Smurf's moralizing, Greedy Smurf's gluttony. Speaking of which, that very day, at the forest's edge...
HEY LOOK at those berries! I've never smurfed anything like them!
They look delicious!
Don't touch that! It's dangerous! Papa Smurf always says that we must mistrust what we don't know!
I don't smurf what Papa Smurf says!
SCRUNCH
Oh! I'll tell him!
Whooaaa! What's happening? My stomach hurts!
See?! I'd warned you!
I'm so SICK!
Oh, my! We have to get you to bed!
Here! First, drink this big glass of bicarbosmurf of sodium! And then I'll give you a little shot! Afterwards, I'll--
Ow! I'll tell Papa Smurf you don't want me to care for you!
SLAM
1
Peyo

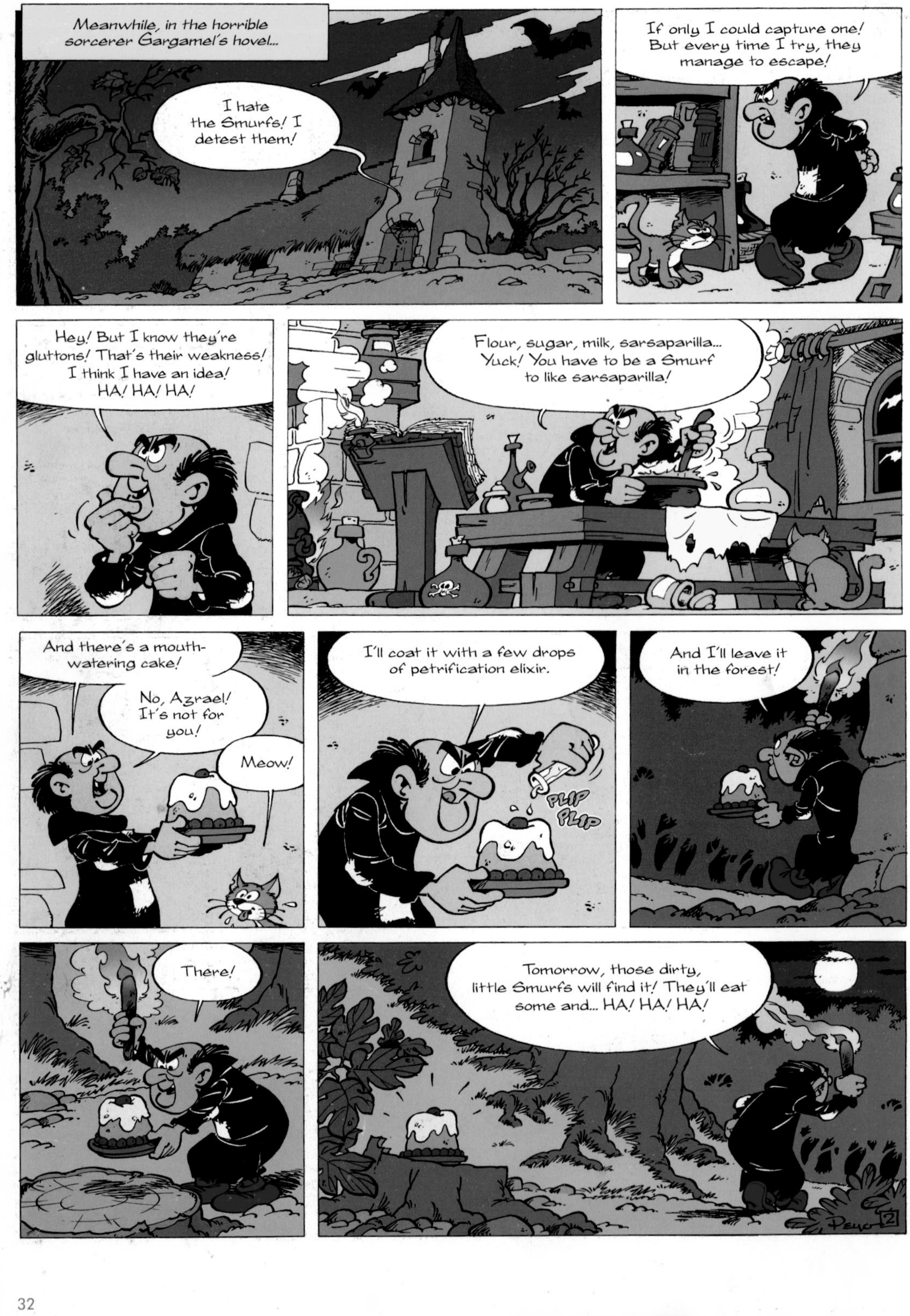
Meanwhile, in the horrible sorcerer Gargamel's hovel...
I hate the Smurfs! I detest them!
If only I could capture one! But every time I try, they manage to escape!
Hey! But I know they're gluttons! That's their weakness! I think I have an idea! HA! HA! HA!
Flour, sugar, milk, sarsaparilla... Yuck! You have to be a Smurf to like sarsaparilla!
And there's a mouth-watering cake!
No, Azrael! It's not for you!
Meow!
I'll coat it with a few drops of petrification elixir.
PLIP PLIP
And I'll leave it in the forest!
There!
Tomorrow, those dirty, little Smurfs will find it! They'll eat some and... HA! HA! HA!
2

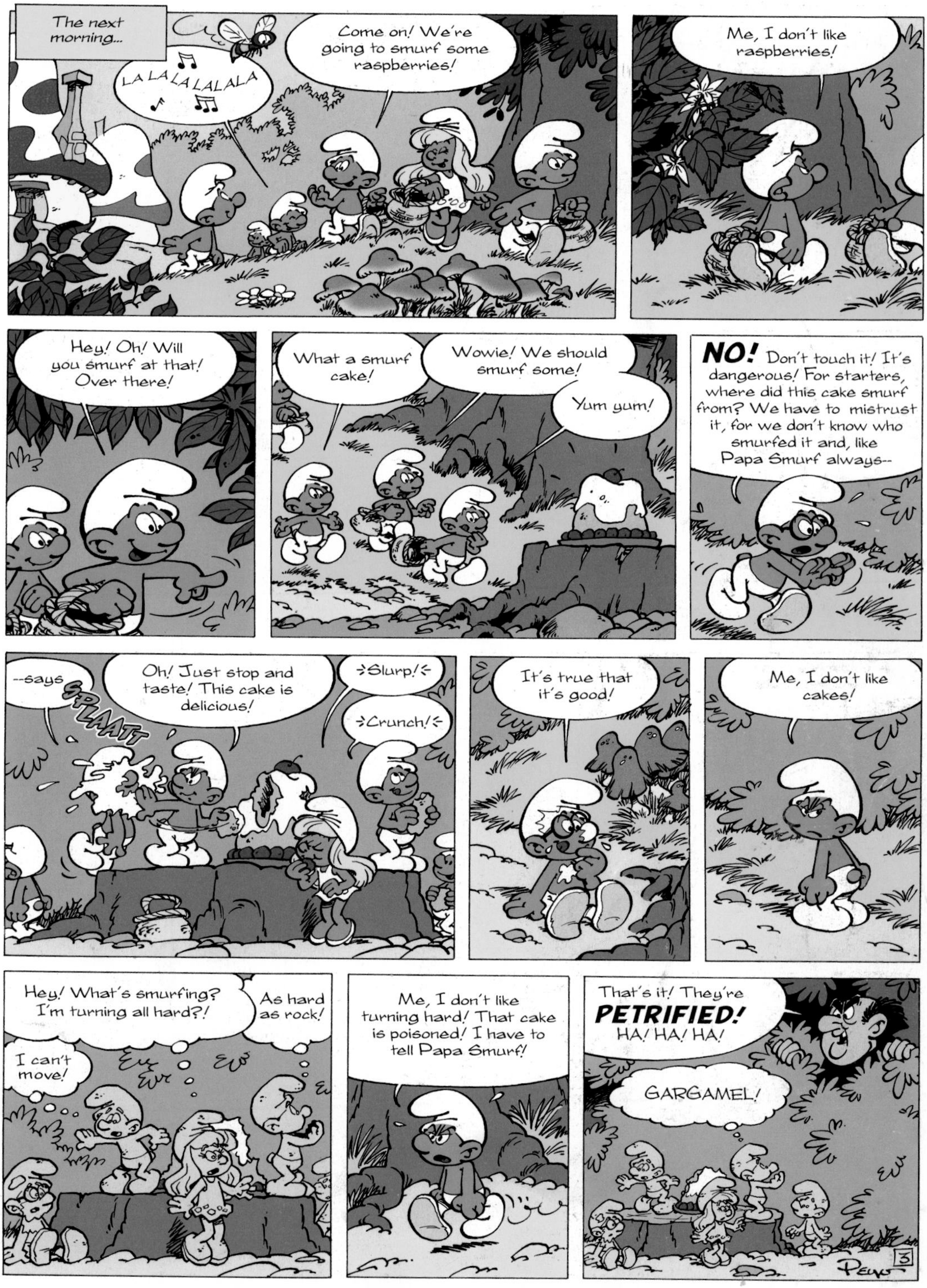
The next morning...
LA LA LA LALALA
Come on! We're going to smurf some raspberries!
Me, I don't like raspberries!
Hey! Oh! Will you smurf at that! Over there!
What a smurf cake!
Wowie! We should smurf some!
Yum yum!
NO! Don't touch it! It's dangerous! For starters, where did this cake smurf from? We have to mistrust it, for we don't know who smurfed it and, like Papa Smurf always--
--says
SPLAATT
Oh! Just stop and taste! This cake is delicious!
Slurp!
Crunch!
It's true that it's good!
Me, I don't like cakes!
Hey! What's smurfing? I'm turning all hard?!
As hard as rock!
I can't move!
Me, I don't like turning hard! That cake is poisoned! I have to tell Papa Smurf!
That's it! They're PETRIFIED! HA! HA! HA!
GARGAMEL!
3
PEYO

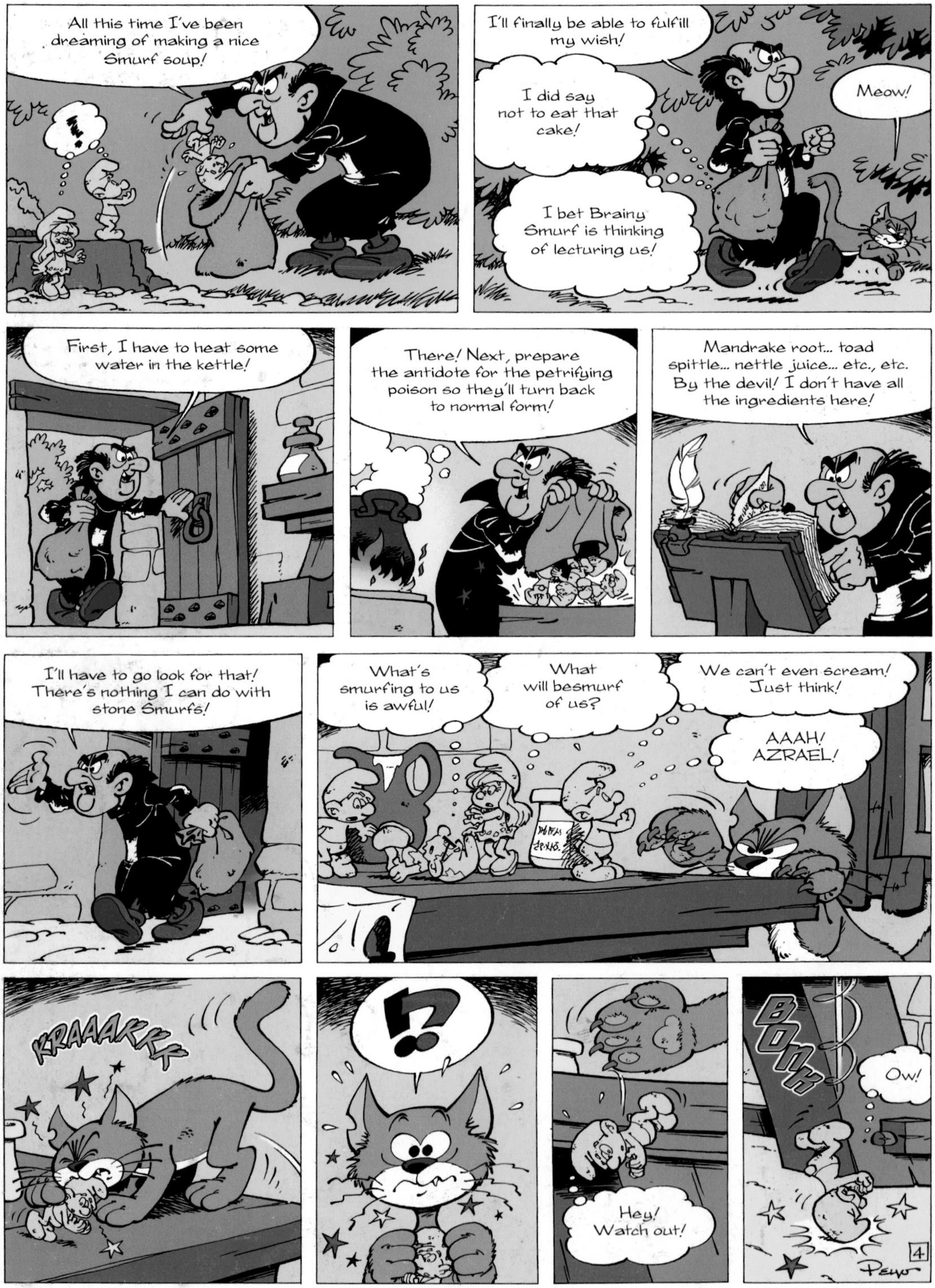
All this time I've been dreaming of making a nice Smurf soup!
!
I'll finally be able to fulfill my wish!
I did say not to eat that cake!
I bet Brainy Smurf is thinking of lecturing us!
Meow!
First, I have to heat some water in the kettle!
There! Next, prepare the antidote for the petrifying poison so they'll turn back to normal form!
Mandrake root... toad spittle... nettle juice... etc., etc. By the devil! I don't have all the ingredients here!
I'll have to go look for that! There's nothing I can do with stone Smurfs!
What's smurfing to us is awful!
What will besmurf of us?
We can't even scream! Just think!
AAAH! AZRAEL!
KRAAARKKK
?!
Hey! Watch out!
BONK
Ow!
4
Peyo

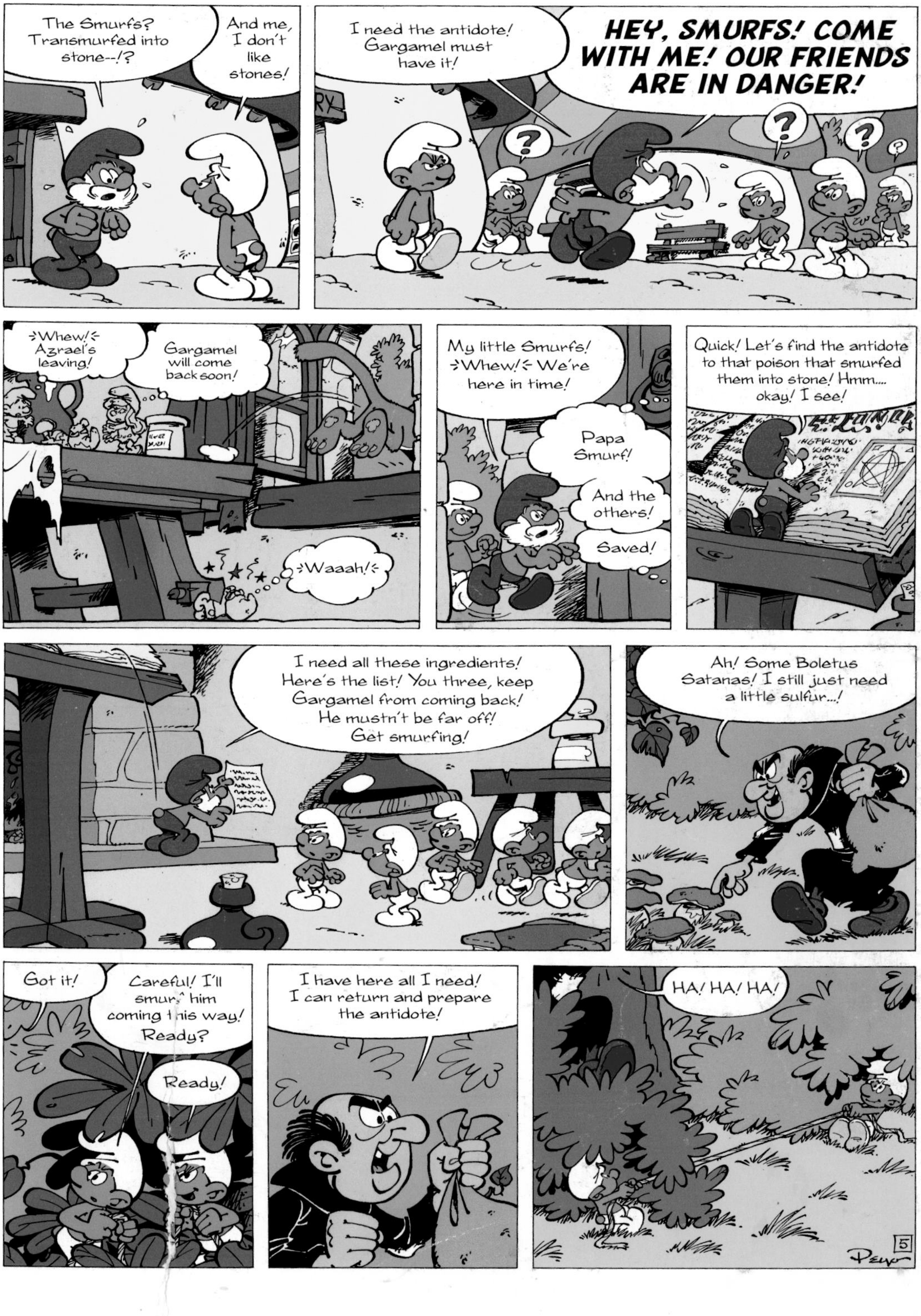

The Smurfs? Transmurfed into stone--!?
And me, I don't like stones!
I need the antidote! Gargamel must have it!
HEY, SMURFS! COME WITH ME! OUR FRIENDS ARE IN DANGER!
Whew! Azrael's leaving!
Gargamel will come back soon!
Waaah!
My little Smurfs! Whew! We're here in time!
Papa Smurf!
And the others!
Saved!
Quick! Let's find the antidote to that poison that smurfed them into stone! Hmm.... okay! I see!
I need all these ingredients! Here's the list! You three, keep Gargamel from coming back! He mustn't be far off! Get smurfing!
Ah! Some Boletus Satanas! I still just need a little sulfur...!
Got it!
Careful! I'll smurf him coming this way! Ready?
Ready!
I have here all I need! I can return and prepare the antidote!
HA! HA! HA!
5

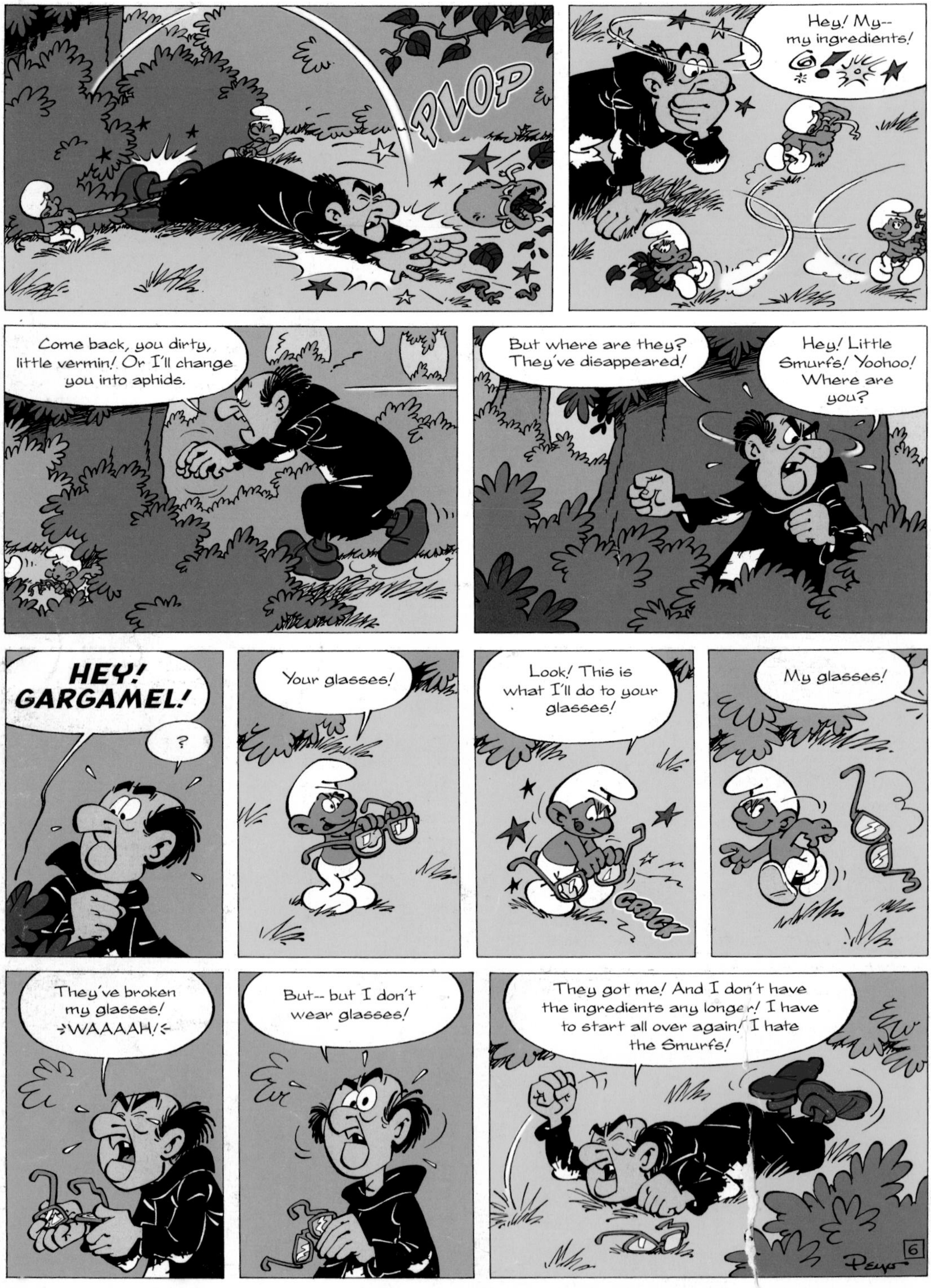
PLOP
Hey! My-- my ingredients!
Come back, you dirty, little vermin! Or I'll change you into aphids.
But where are they? They've disappeared!
Hey! Little Smurfs! Yoohoo! Where are you?
HEY! GARGAMEL!
?
Your glasses!
Look! This is what I'll do to your glasses!
CRACK
My glasses!
They've broken my glasses! WAAAAH!
But-- but I don't wear glasses!
They got me! And I don't have the ingredients any longer! I have to start all over again! I hate the Smurfs!
6
Peyo

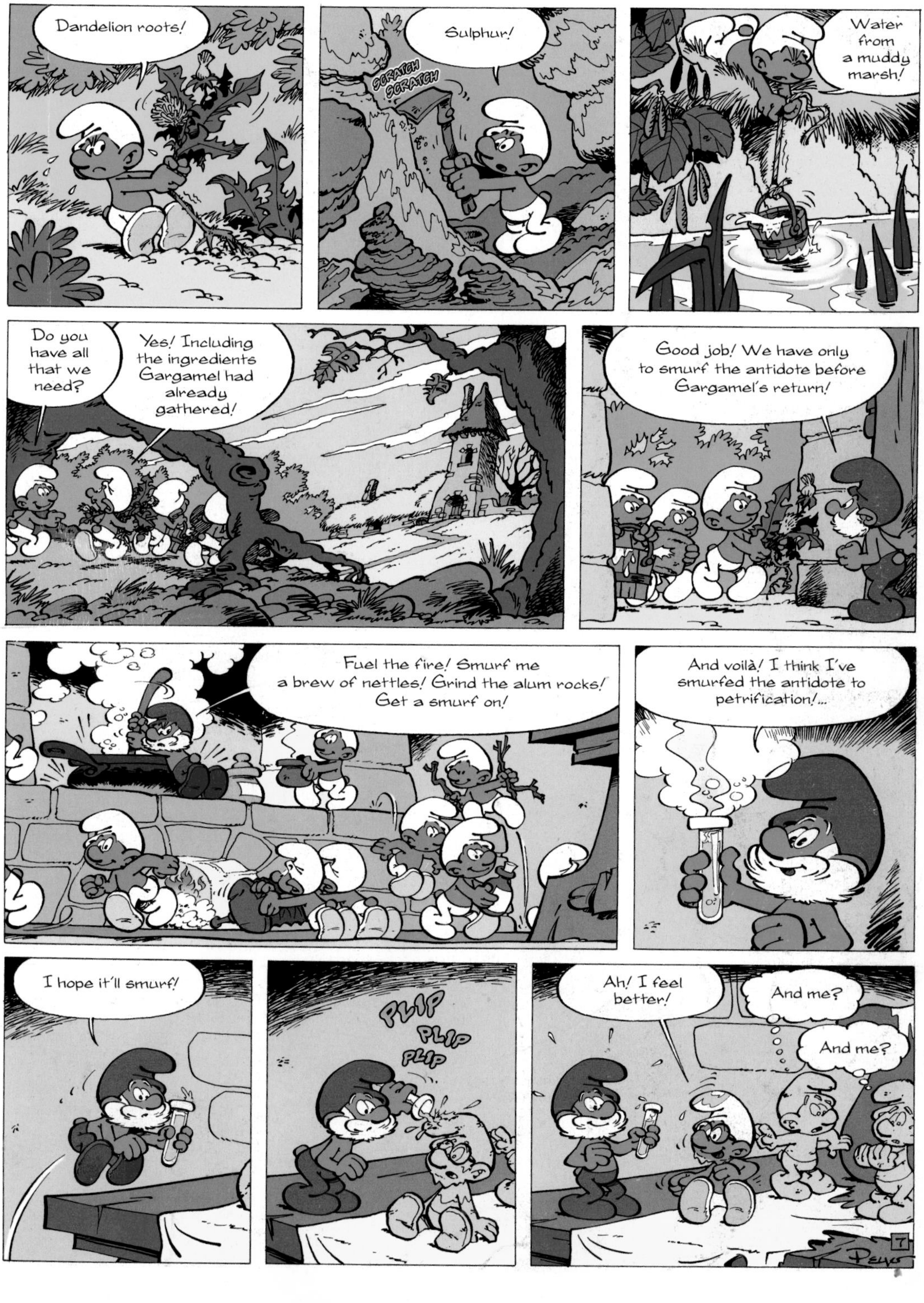

Dandelion roots!
SCRATCH SCRATCH
Sulphur!
Water from a muddy marsh!
Do you have all that we need?
Yes! Including the ingredients Gargamel had already gathered!
Good job! We have only to smurf the antidote before Gargamel's return!
Fuel the fire! Smurf me a brew of nettles! Grind the alum rocks! Get a smurf on!
And voilà! I think I've smurfed the antidote to petrification!...
I hope it'll smurf!
PLIP
PLIP
PLIP
Ah! I feel better!
And me?
And me?
7

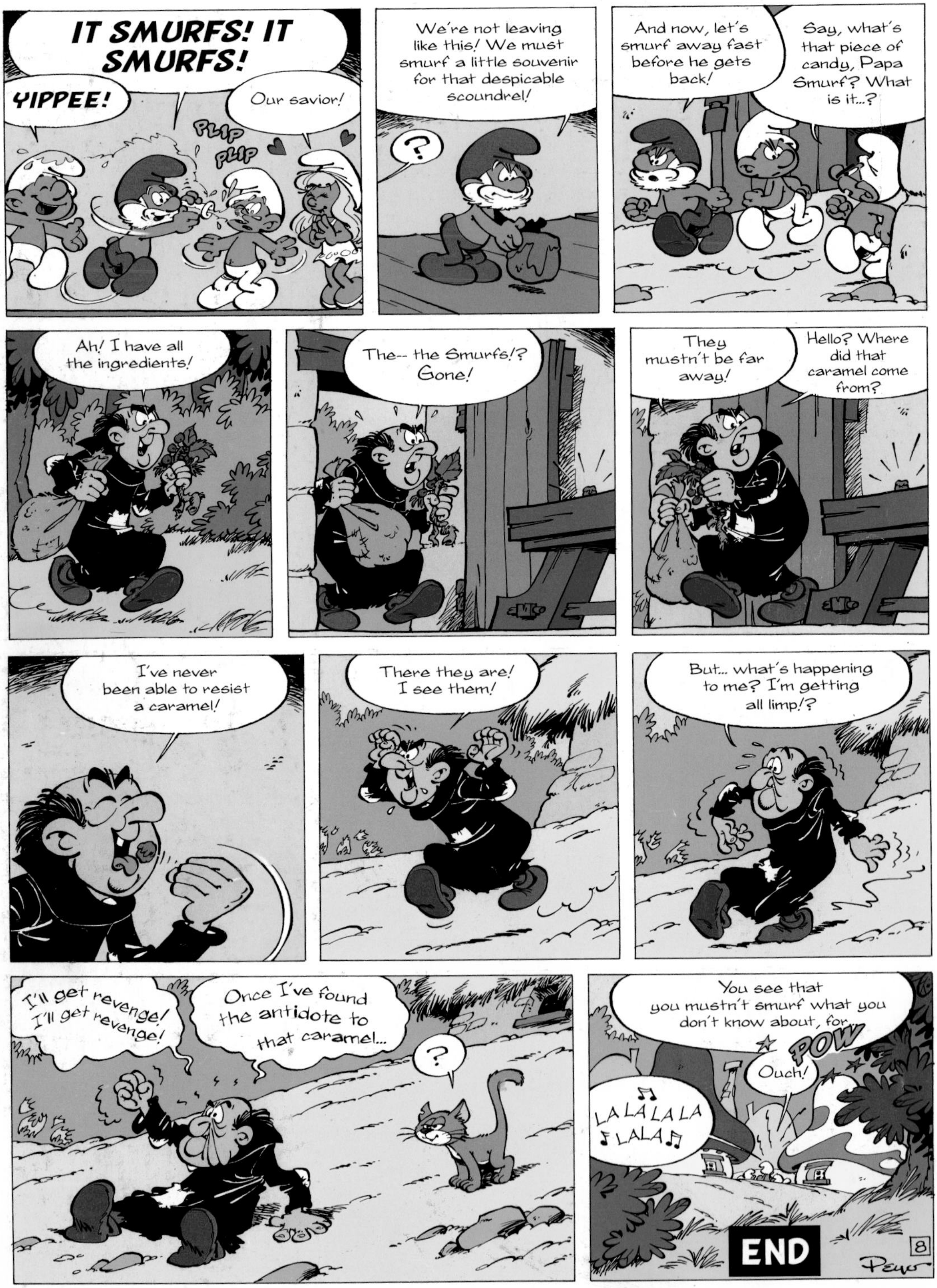
IT SMURFS! IT SMURFS!
YIPPEE!
Our savior!
PLIP PLIP
We're not leaving like this! We must smurf a little souvenir for that despicable scoundrel!
?
And now, let's smurf away fast before he gets back!
Say, what's that piece of candy, Papa Smurf? What is it...?
Ah! I have all the ingredients!
The-- the Smurfs!? Gone!
They mustn't be far away!
Hello? Where did that caramel come from?
I've never been able to resist a caramel!
There they are! I see them!
But... what's happening to me? I'm getting all limp!?
I'll get revenge! I'll get revenge!
Once I've found the antidote to that caramel...
?
You see that you mustn't smurf what you don't know about, for...
POW
Ouch!
LA LA LA LA LA LA LA
END
8
Peyo

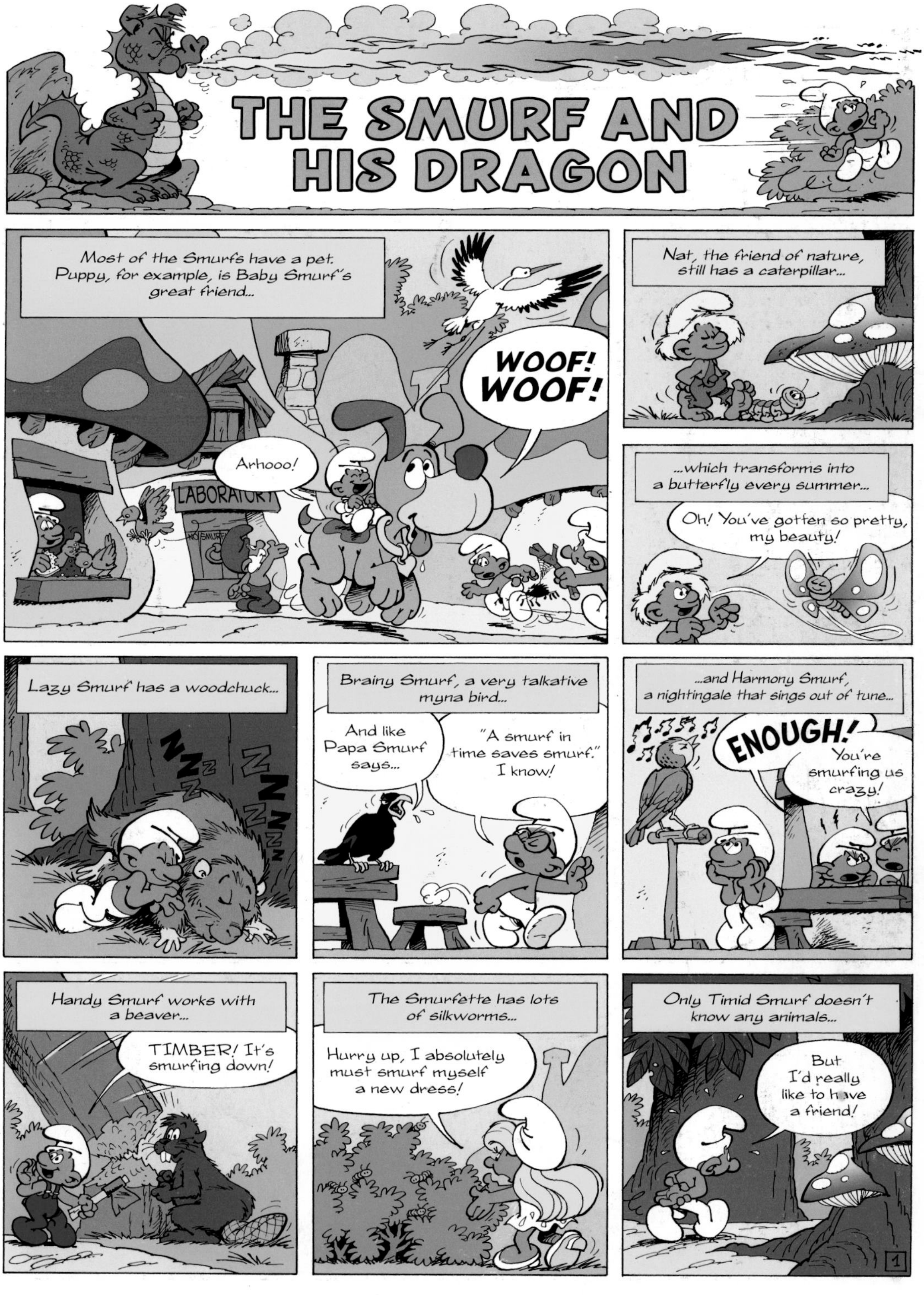
THE SMURF AND HIS DRAGON
Most of the Smurfs have a pet. Puppy, for example, is Baby Smurf's great friend...
WOOF! WOOF!
Arhooo!
LABORATORY
Nat, the friend of nature, still has a caterpillar...
...which transforms into a butterfly every summer...
Oh! You've gotten so pretty, my beauty!
Lazy Smurf has a woodchuck...
ZZZ ZZZZZ
Brainy Smurf, a very talkative myna bird...
And like Papa Smurf says...
"A smurf in time saves smurf." I know!
...and Harmony Smurf, a nightingale that sings out of tune...
ENOUGH!
You're smurfing us crazy!
Handy Smurf works with a beaver...
TIMBER! It's smurfing down!
The Smurfette has lots of silkworms...
Hurry up, I absolutely must smurf myself a new dress!
Only Timid Smurf doesn't know any animals...
But I'd really like to have a friend!
1

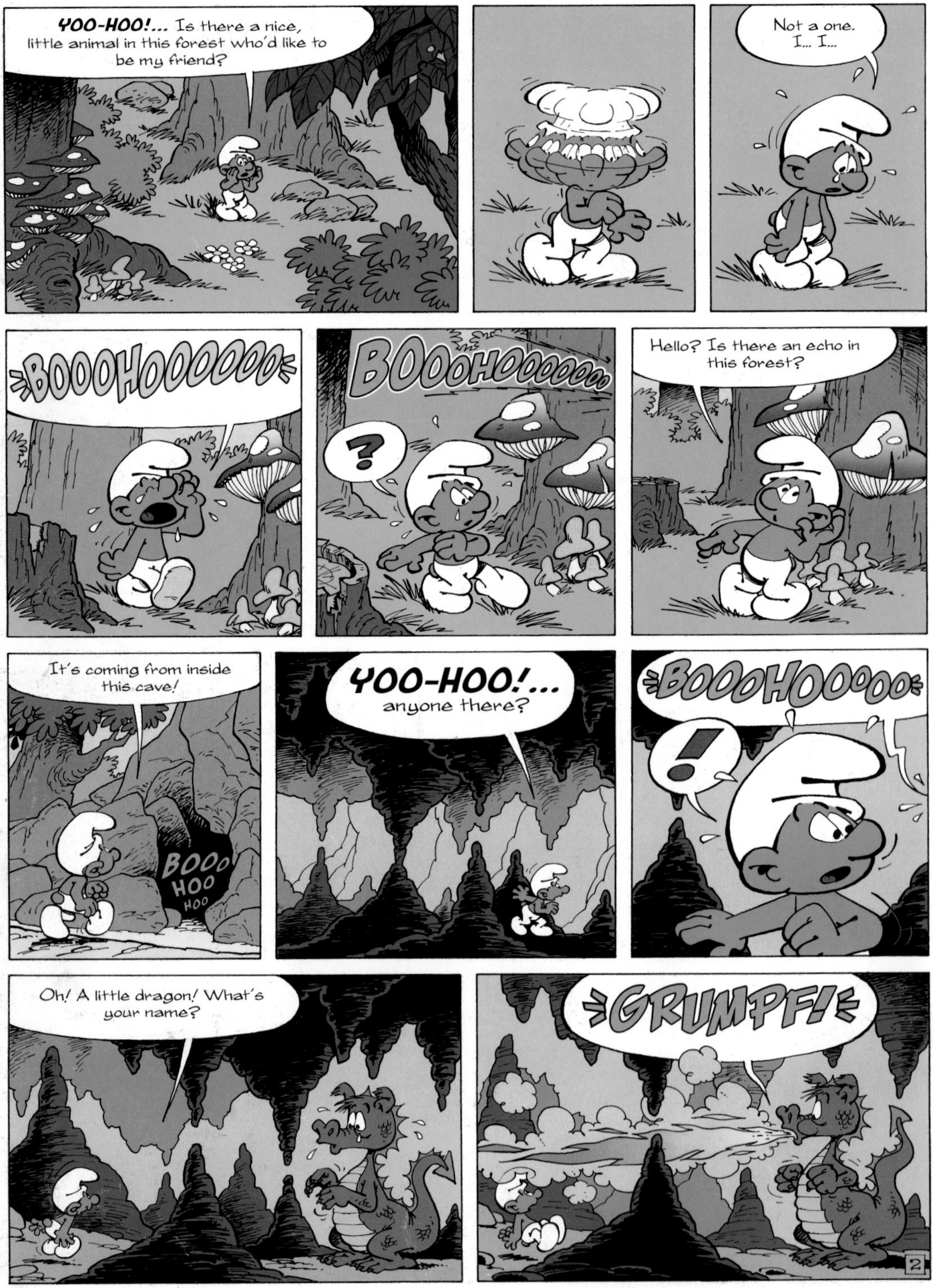
YOO-HOO!... Is there a nice, little animal in this forest who'd like to be my friend?
Not a one. I... I...
BOOOHOOOOOO
BOOoHOOooooo
?
Hello? Is there an echo in this forest?
It's coming from inside this cave!
BOOO HOO HOO
YOO-HOO!... anyone there?
BOOOHOOoOO
!
Oh! A little dragon! What's your name?
GRUMPF!
2

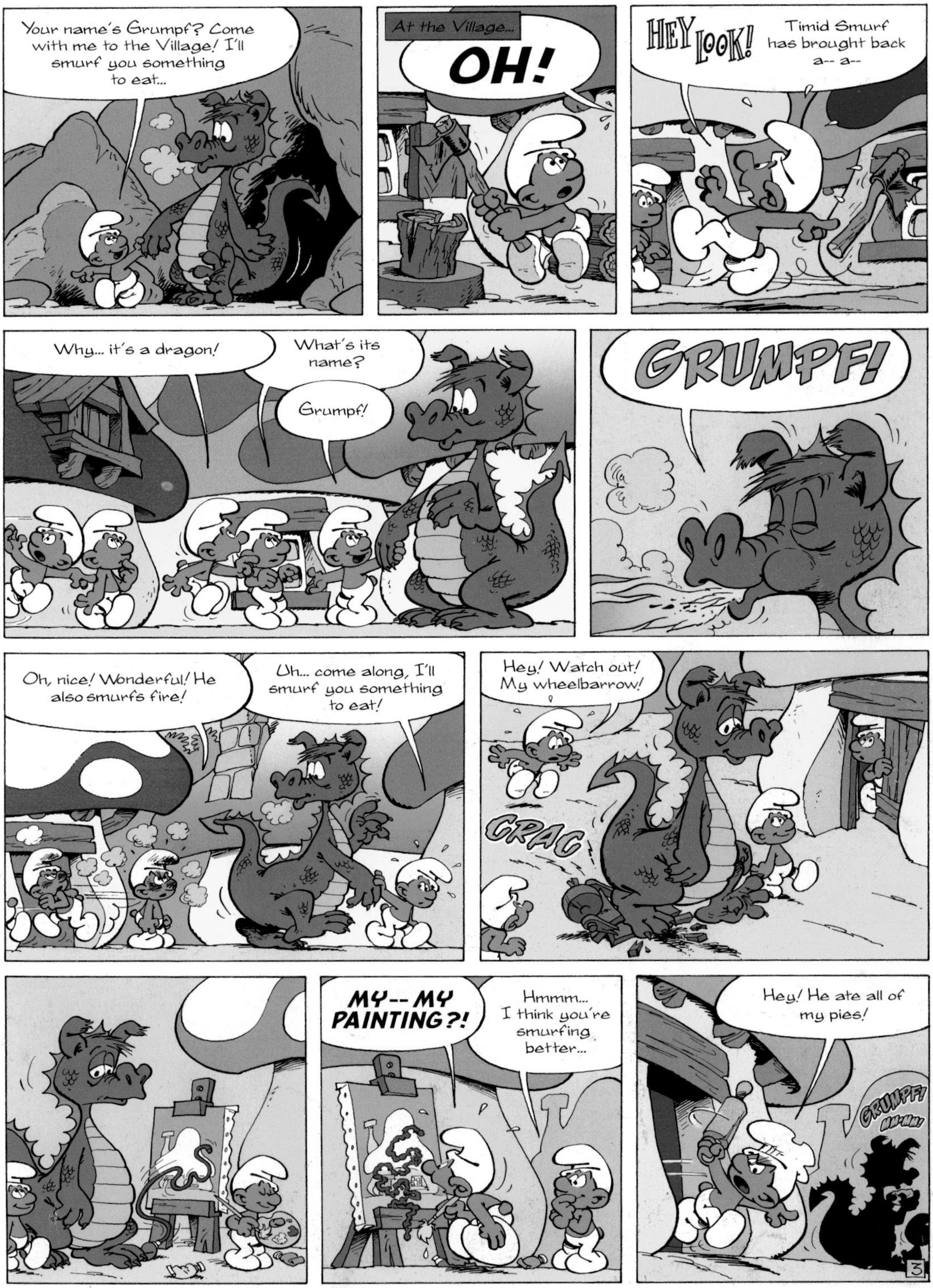
Your name's Grumpf? Come with me to the Village! I'll smurf you something to eat...
At the Village...
OH!
HEY LOOK!
Timid Smurf has brought back a-- a--
Why... it's a dragon!
What's its name?
Grumpf!
GRUMPF!
Oh, nice! Wonderful! He also smurfs fire!
Uh... come along, I'll smurf you something to eat!
Hey! Watch out! My wheelbarrow!
CRAC
MY-- MY PAINTING?!
Hmmm... I think you're smurfing better...
Hey! He ate all of my pies!
GRUMPF!
3

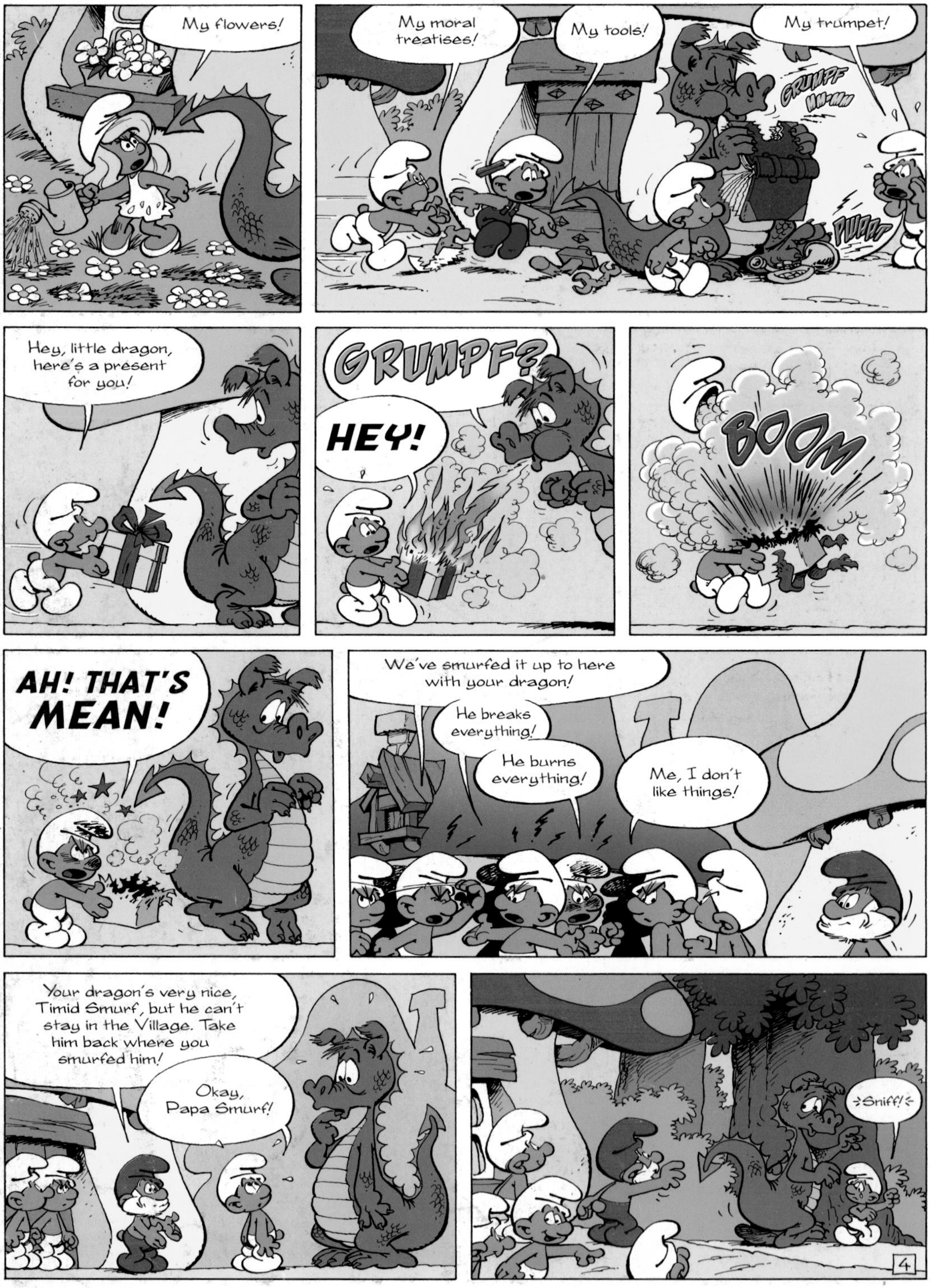

My flowers!
My moral treatises!
My tools!
GRUMPF
MM-MM
My trumpet!
PUUOT
Hey, little dragon, here's a present for you!
GRUMPF?
HEY!
BOOM
AH! THAT'S MEAN!
We've smurfed it up to here with your dragon!
He breaks everything!
He burns everything!
Me, I don't like things!
Your dragon's very nice, Timid Smurf, but he can't stay in the Village. Take him back where you smurfed him!
Okay, Papa Smurf!
Sniff!
4

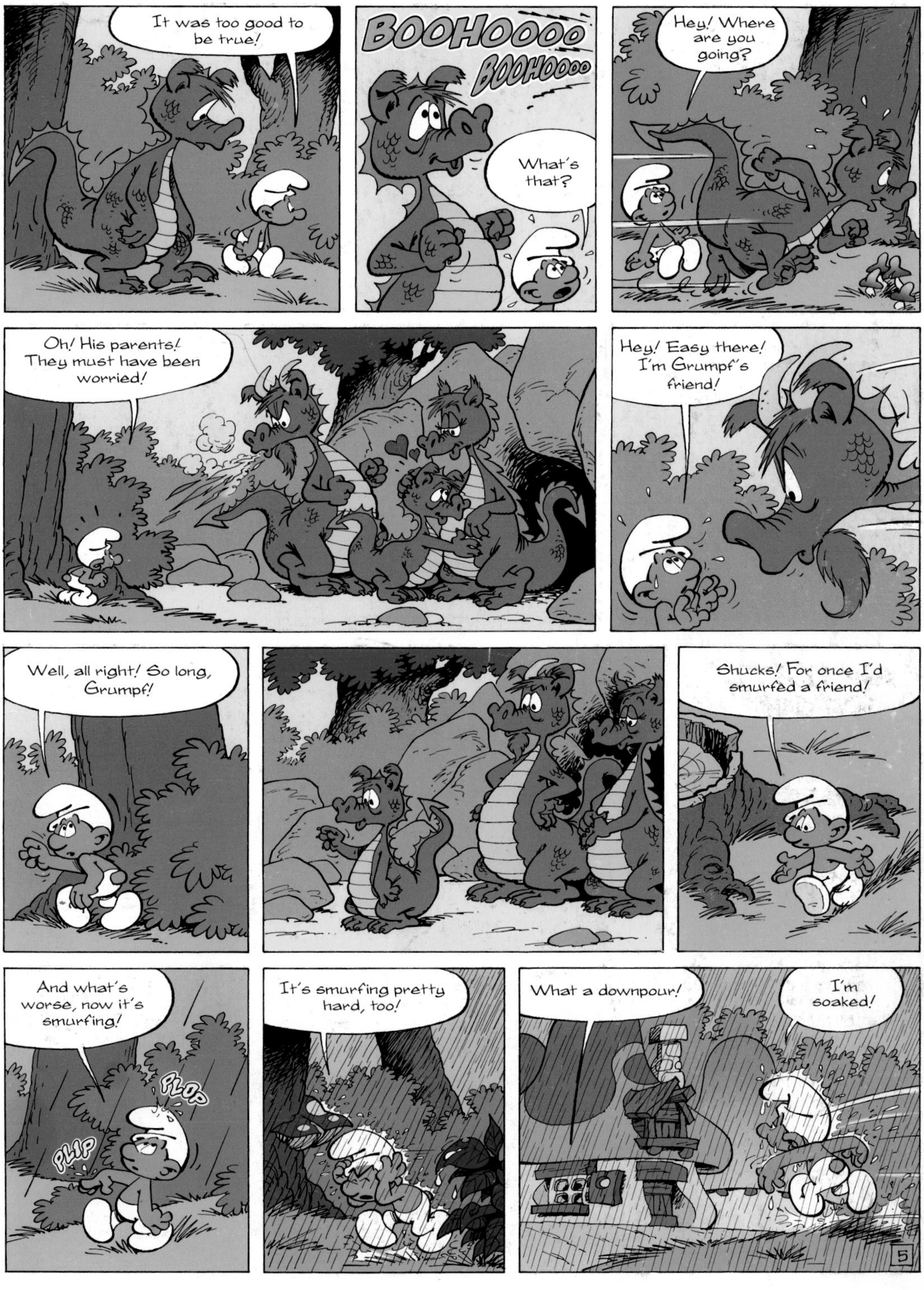
It was too good to be true!
BOOHOOOO
BOOHOOOO
What's that?
Hey! Where are you going?
Oh! His parents! They must have been worried!
Hey! Easy there! I'm Grumpf's friend!
Well, all right! So long, Grumpf!
Shucks! For once I'd smurfed a friend!
And what's worse, now it's smurfing!
PLOP
PLIP
It's smurfing pretty hard, too!
What a downpour!
I'm soaked!
5

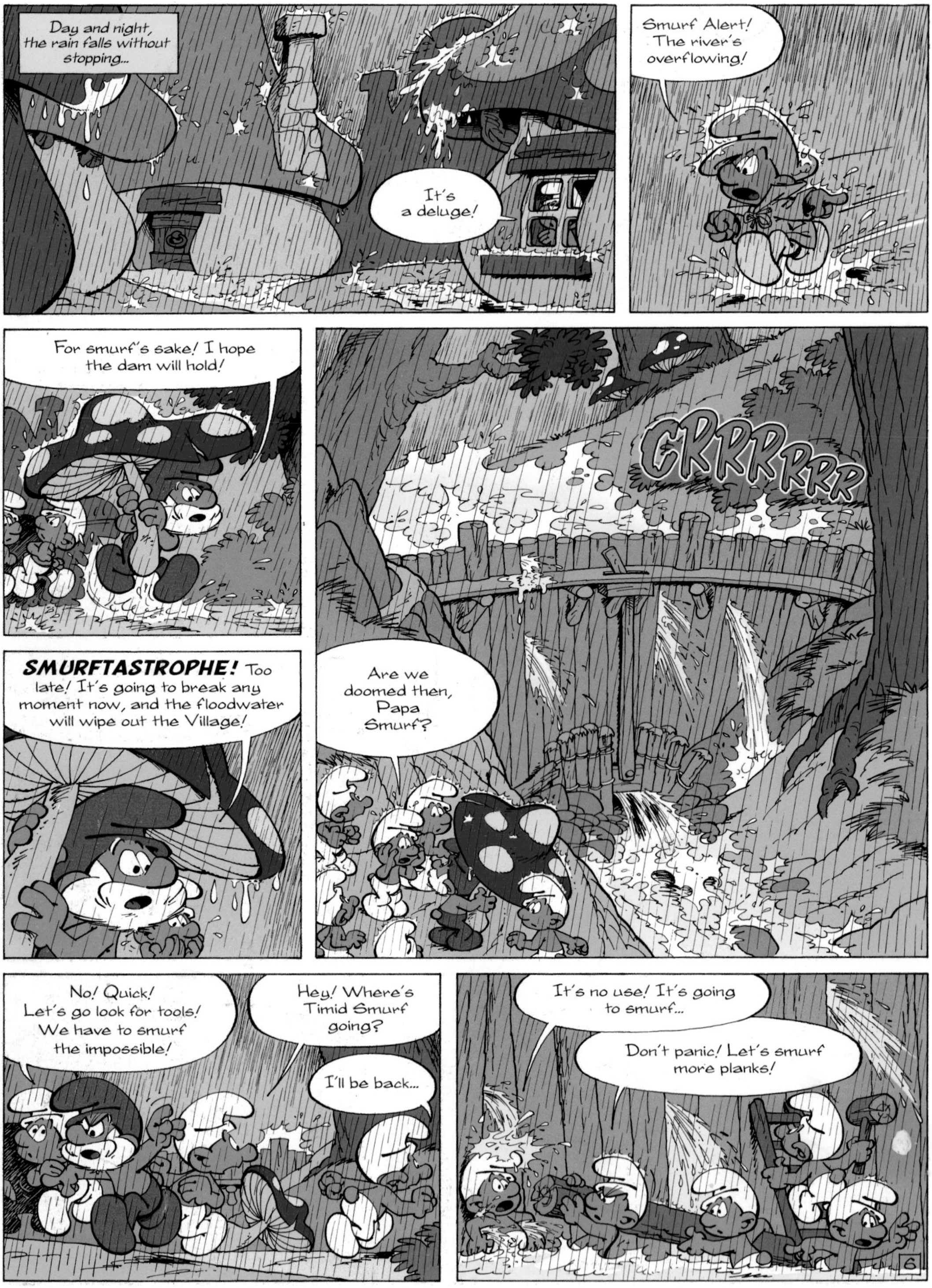
Day and night, the rain falls without stopping...
It's a deluge!
Smurf Alert! The river's overflowing!
For smurf's sake! I hope the dam will hold!
GRRRRRR
SMURFTASTROPHE! Too late! It's going to break any moment now, and the floodwater will wipe out the Village!
Are we doomed then, Papa Smurf?
No! Quick! Let's go look for tools! We have to smurf the impossible!
Hey! Where's Timid Smurf going?
I'll be back...
It's no use! It's going to smurf...
Don't panic! Let's smurf more planks!
6

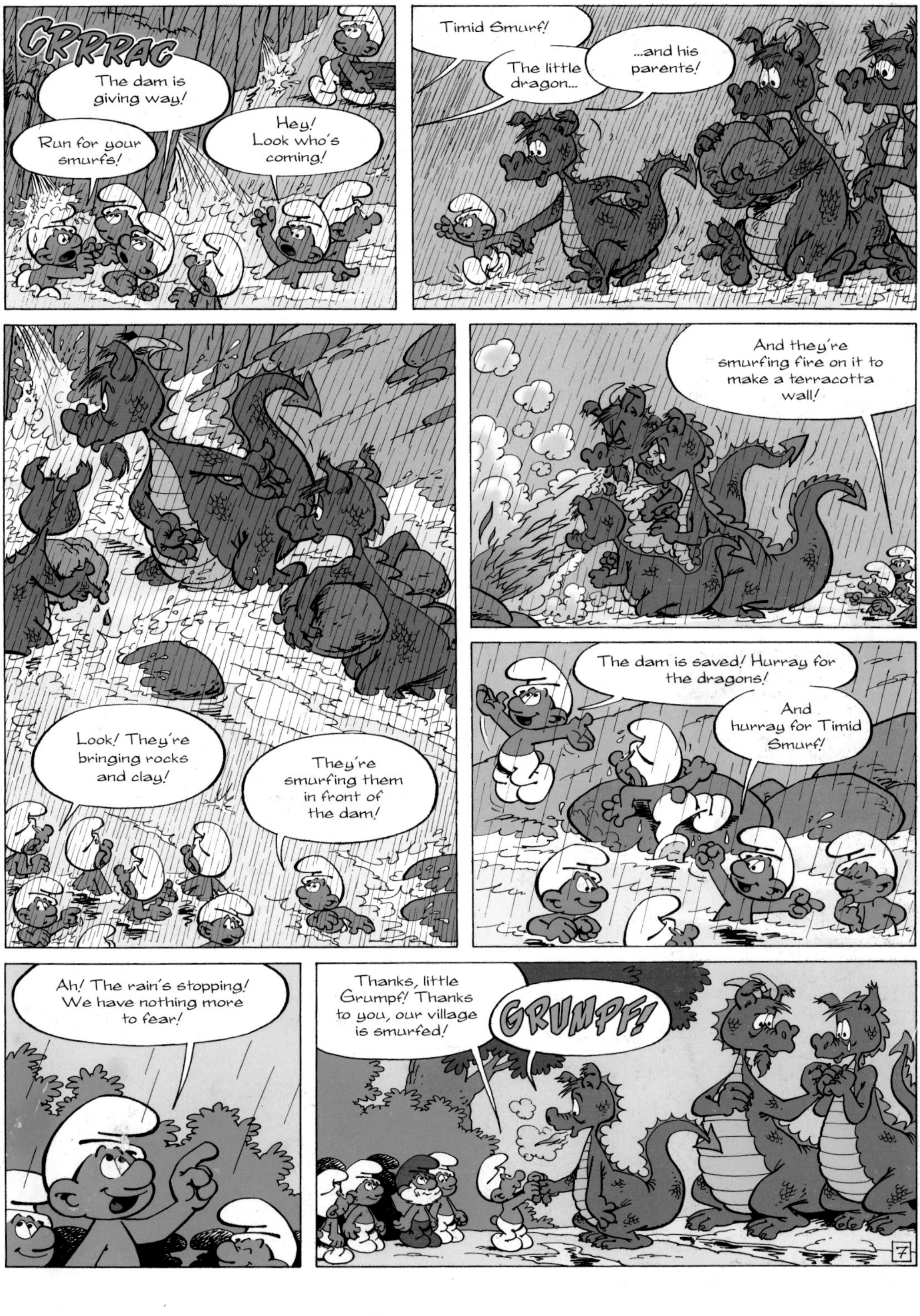

GRRRAC
The dam is giving way!
Run for your smurfs!
Hey! Look who's coming!
Timid Smurf!
The little dragon...
...and his parents!
Look! They're bringing rocks and clay!
They're smurfing them in front of the dam!
And they're smurfing fire on it to make a terracotta wall!
The dam is saved! Hurray for the dragons!
And hurray for Timid Smurf!
Ah! The rain's stopping! We have nothing more to fear!
Thanks, little Grumpf! Thanks to you, our village is smurfed!
GRUMPF!
7

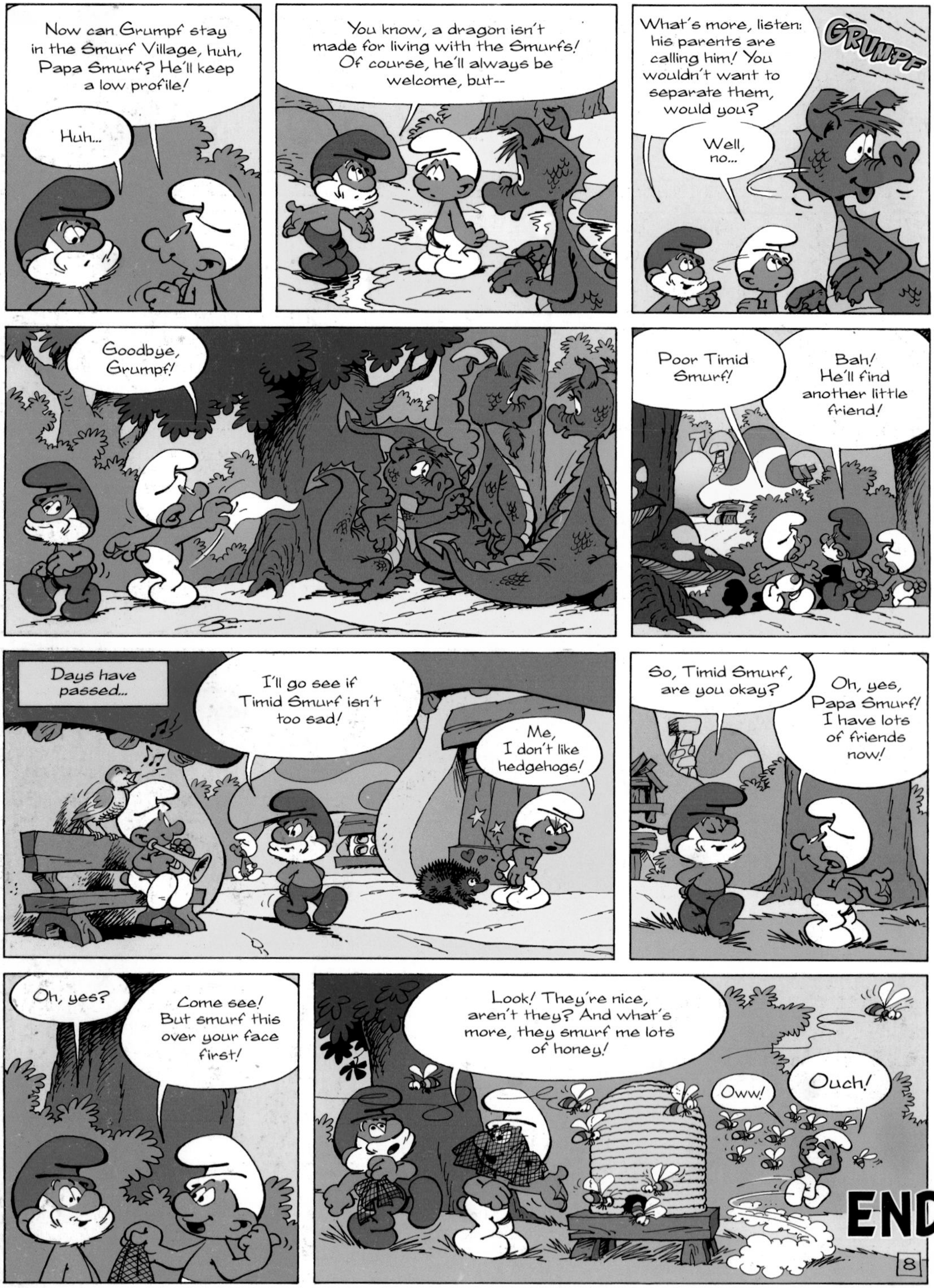
Now can Grumpf stay in the Smurf Village, huh, Papa Smurf? He'll keep a low profile!
Huh...
You know, a dragon isn't made for living with the Smurfs! Of course, he'll always be welcome, but--
What's more, listen: his parents are calling him! You wouldn't want to separate them, would you?
Well, no...
GRUMPF
Goodbye, Grumpf!
Poor Timid Smurf!
Bah! He'll find another little friend!
Days have passed...
I'll go see if Timid Smurf isn't too sad!
Me, I don't like hedgehogs!
So, Timid Smurf, are you okay?
Oh, yes, Papa Smurf! I have lots of friends now!
Oh, yes?
Come see! But smurf this over your face first!
Look! They're nice, aren't they? And what's more, they smurf me lots of honey!
Oww!
Ouch!
END
8

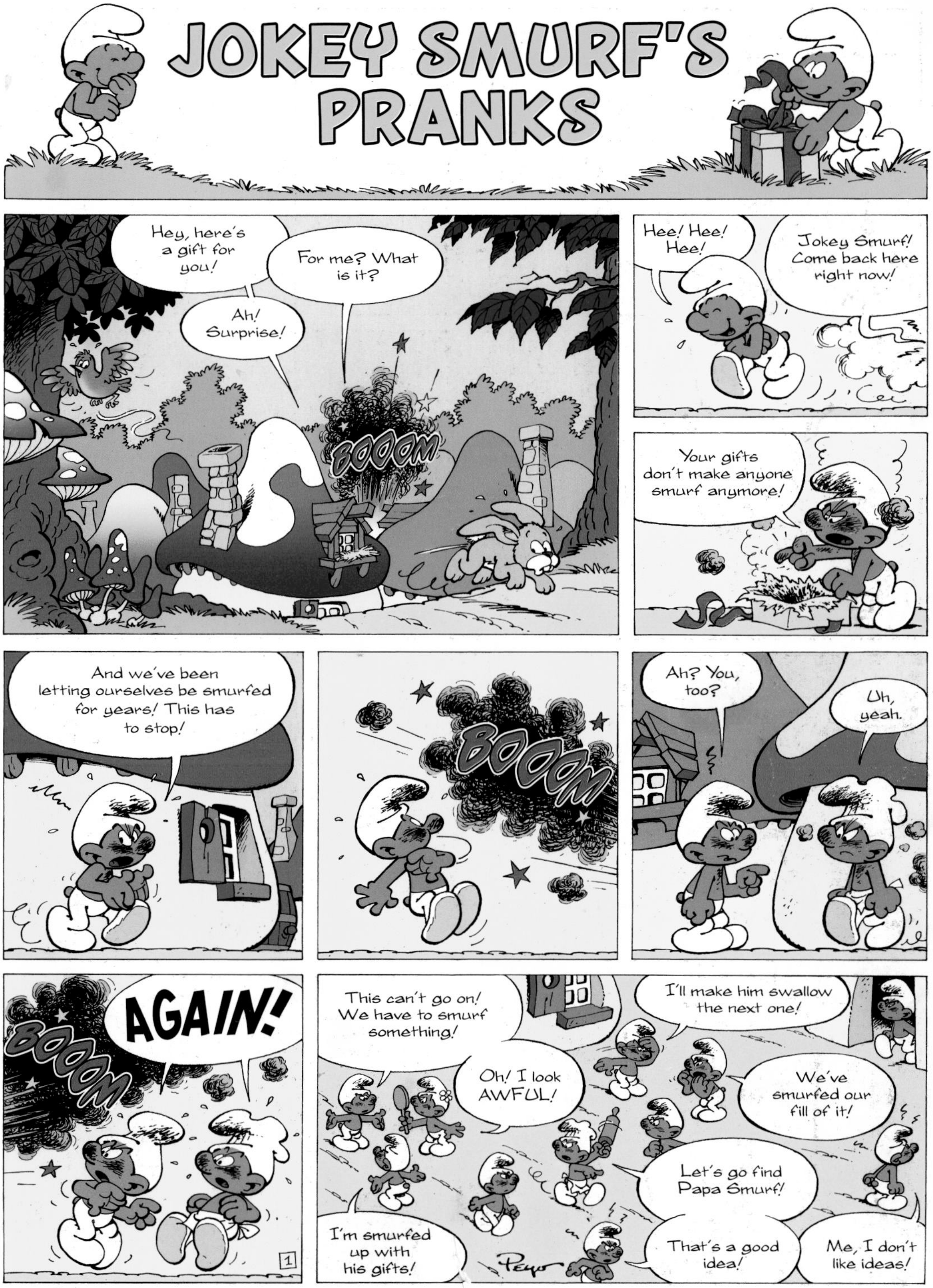

JOKEY SMURF'S PRANKS
Hey, here's a gift for you!
Ah! Surprise!
For me? What is it?
BOOOM
Hee! Hee! Hee!
Jokey Smurf! Come back here right now!
Your gifts don't make anyone smurf anymore!
And we've been letting ourselves be smurfed for years! This has to stop!
BOOOM
Ah? You, too?
Uh, yeah.
BOOOM
AGAIN!
1
This can't go on! We have to smurf something!
Oh! I look AWFUL!
I'll make him swallow the next one!
We've smurfed our fill of it!
Let's go find Papa Smurf!
I'm smurfed up with his gifts!
That's a good idea!
Me, I don't like ideas!
Peyo

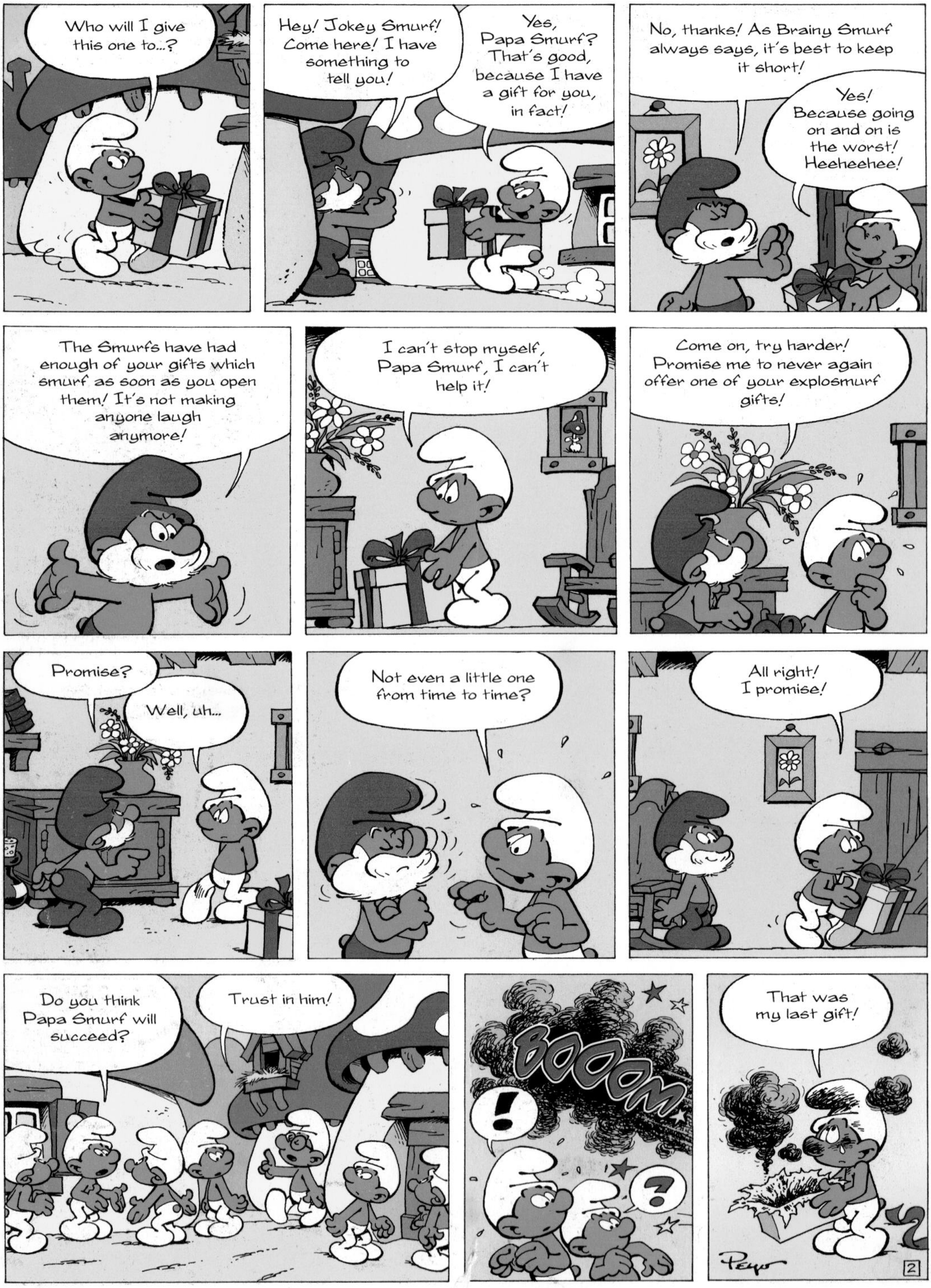
Who will I give this one to...?
Hey! Jokey Smurf! Come here! I have something to tell you!
Yes, Papa Smurf? That's good, because I have a gift for you, in fact!
No, thanks! As Brainy Smurf always says, it's best to keep it short!
Yes! Because going on and on is the worst! Heeheehee!
The Smurfs have had enough of your gifts which smurf as soon as you open them! It's not making anyone laugh anymore!
I can't stop myself, Papa Smurf, I can't help it!
Come on, try harder! Promise me to never again offer one of your explosmurf gifts!
Promise?
Well, uh...
Not even a little one from time to time?
All right! I promise!
Do you think Papa Smurf will succeed?
Trust in him!
BOOOM
!
?
That was my last gift!
Peyo
2

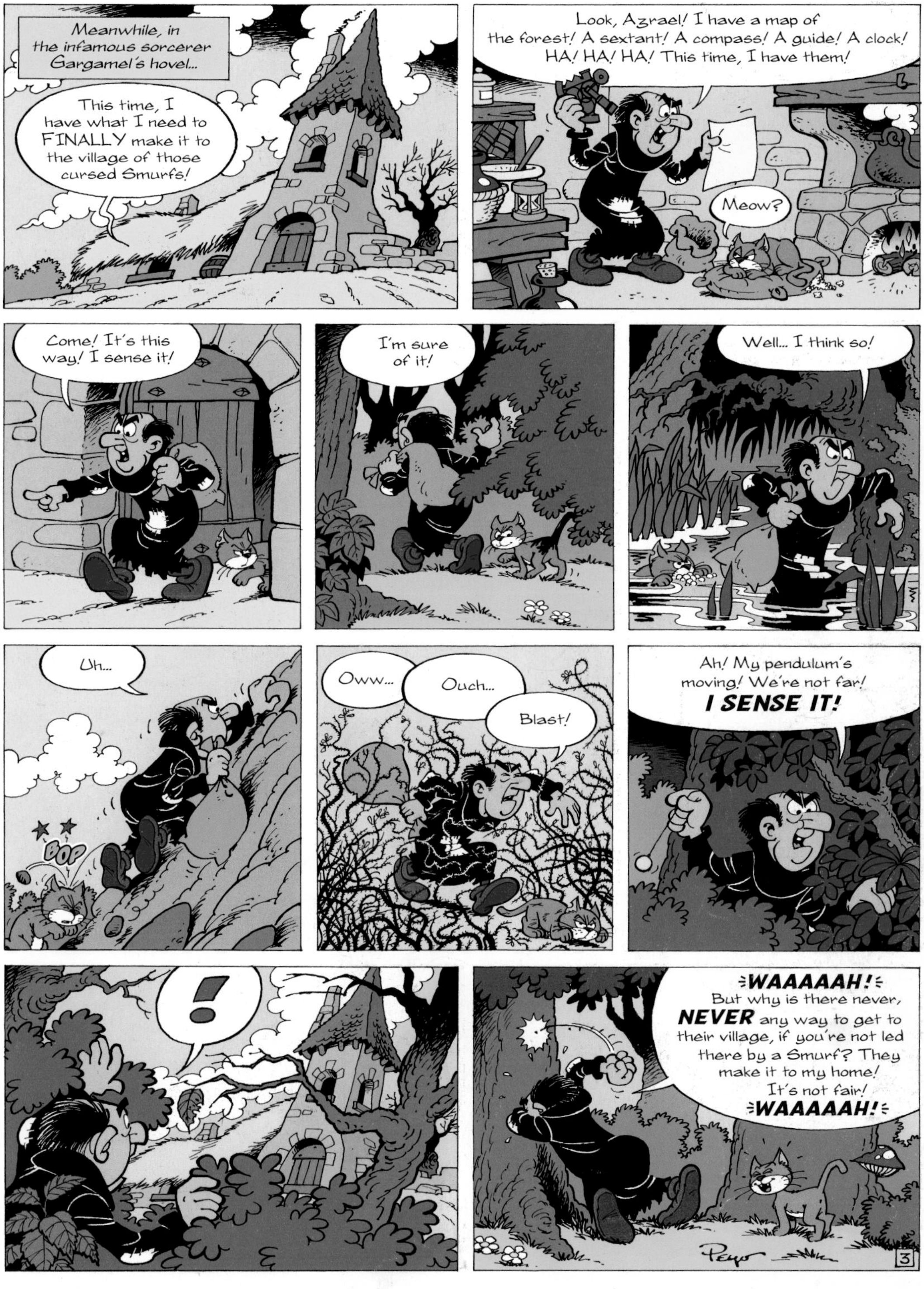
Meanwhile, in the infamous sorcerer Gargamel's hovel...
This time, I have what I need to FINALLY make it to the village of those cursed Smurfs!
Look, Azrael! I have a map of the forest! A sextant! A compass! A guide! A clock! HA! HA! HA! This time, I have them!
Meow?
Come! It's this way! I sense it!
I'm sure of it!
Well... I think so!
Uh...
BOP
Oww...
Ouch...
Blast!
Ah! My pendulum's moving! We're not far! I SENSE IT!
!
WAAAAAH! But why is there never, NEVER any way to get to their village, if you're not led there by a Smurf? They make it to my home! It's not fair! WAAAAAH!
Peyo
3

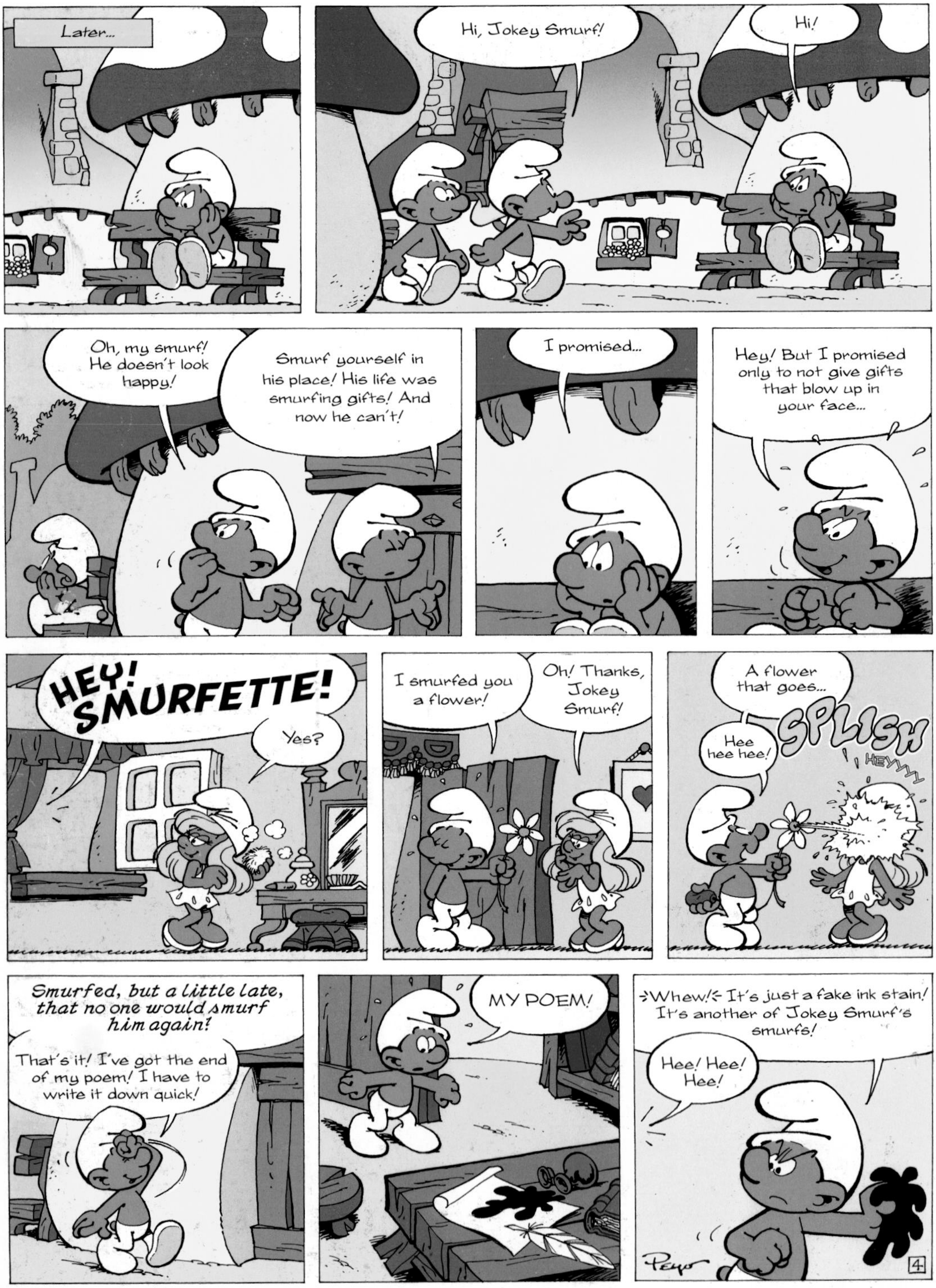
Later...
Hi, Jokey Smurf!
Hi!
Oh, my smurf! He doesn't look happy!
Smurf yourself in his place! His life was smurfing gifts! And now he can't!
I promised...
Hey! But I promised only to not give gifts that blow up in your face...
HEY! SMURFETTE!
Yes?
I smurfed you a flower!
Oh! Thanks, Jokey Smurf!
A flower that goes...
SPLISH
HEYYYY
Hee hee hee!
Smurfed, but a little late, that no one would smurf him again!
That's it! I've got the end of my poem! I have to write it down quick!
MY POEM!
Whew! It's just a fake ink stain! It's another of Jokey Smurf's smurfs!
Hee! Hee! Hee!
Peyo
4

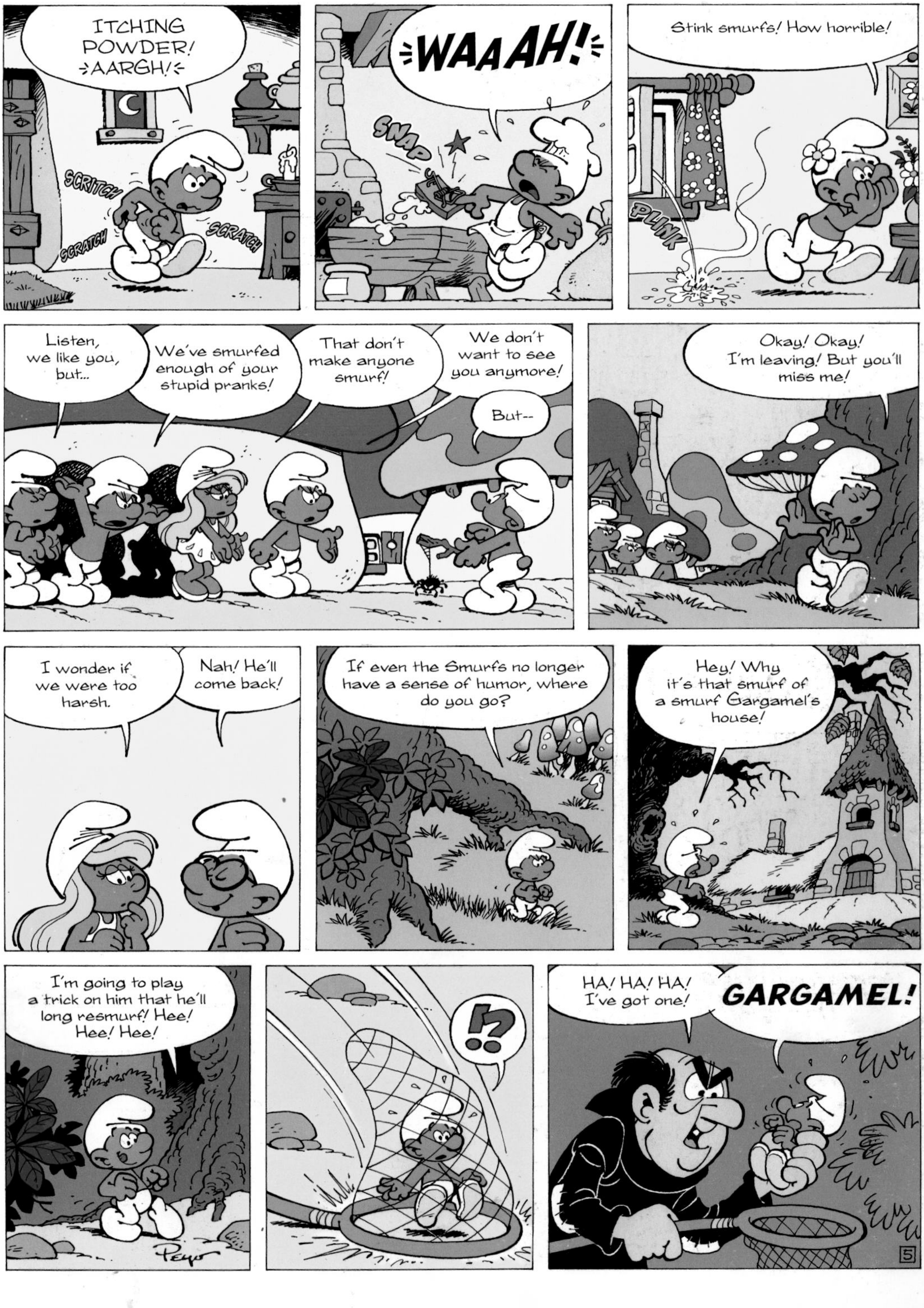
ITCHING POWDER! AARGH!
SCRITCH
SCRATCH
SCRATCH
SNAP
WAAAH!
Stink smurfs! How horrible!
PLINK
Listen, we like you, but...
We've smurfed enough of your stupid pranks!
That don't make anyone smurf!
We don't want to see you anymore!
But--
Okay! Okay! I'm leaving! But you'll miss me!
I wonder if we were too harsh.
Nah! He'll come back!
If even the Smurfs no longer have a sense of humor, where do you go?
Hey! Why it's that smurf of a smurf Gargamel's house!
I'm going to play a trick on him that he'll long resmurf! Hee! Hee! Hee!
!?
HA! HA! HA! I've got one!
GARGAMEL!
Peyo
5

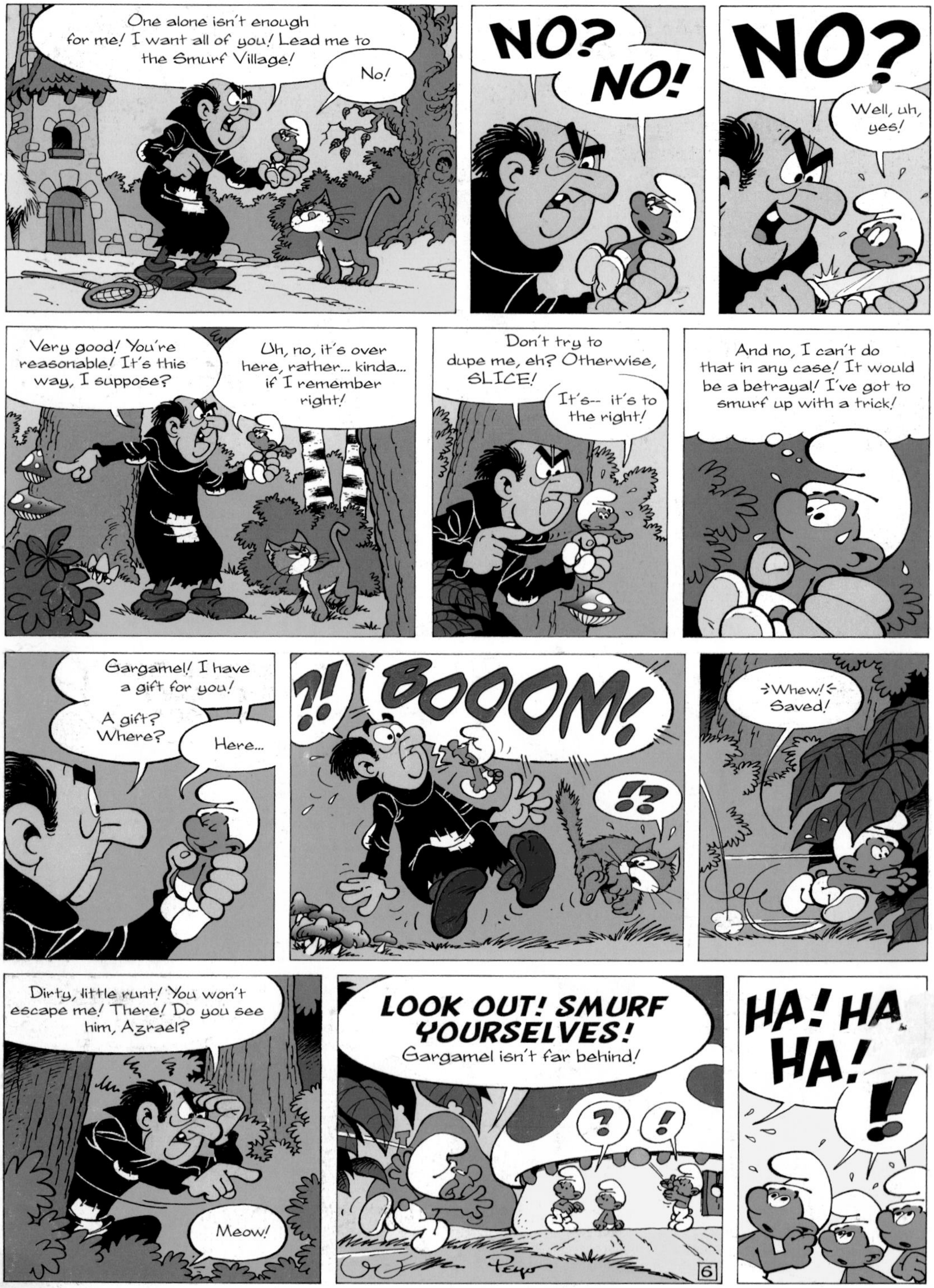

One alone isn't enough for me! I want all of you! Lead me to the Smurf Village!
No!
NO?
NO!
NO?
Well, uh, yes!
Very good! You're reasonable! It's this way, I suppose?
Uh, no, it's over here, rather... kinda... if I remember right!
Don't try to dupe me, eh? Otherwise, SLICE!
It's-- it's to the right!
And no, I can't do that in any case! It would be a betrayal! I've got to smurf up with a trick!
Gargamel! I have a gift for you!
A gift? Where?
Here...
?!
BOOOM!
!?
Whew! Saved!
Dirty, little runt! You won't escape me! There! Do you see him, Azrael?
Meow!
LOOK OUT! SMURF YOURSELVES!
Gargamel isn't far behind!
?
!
Peyo
6
HA! HA HA!
!

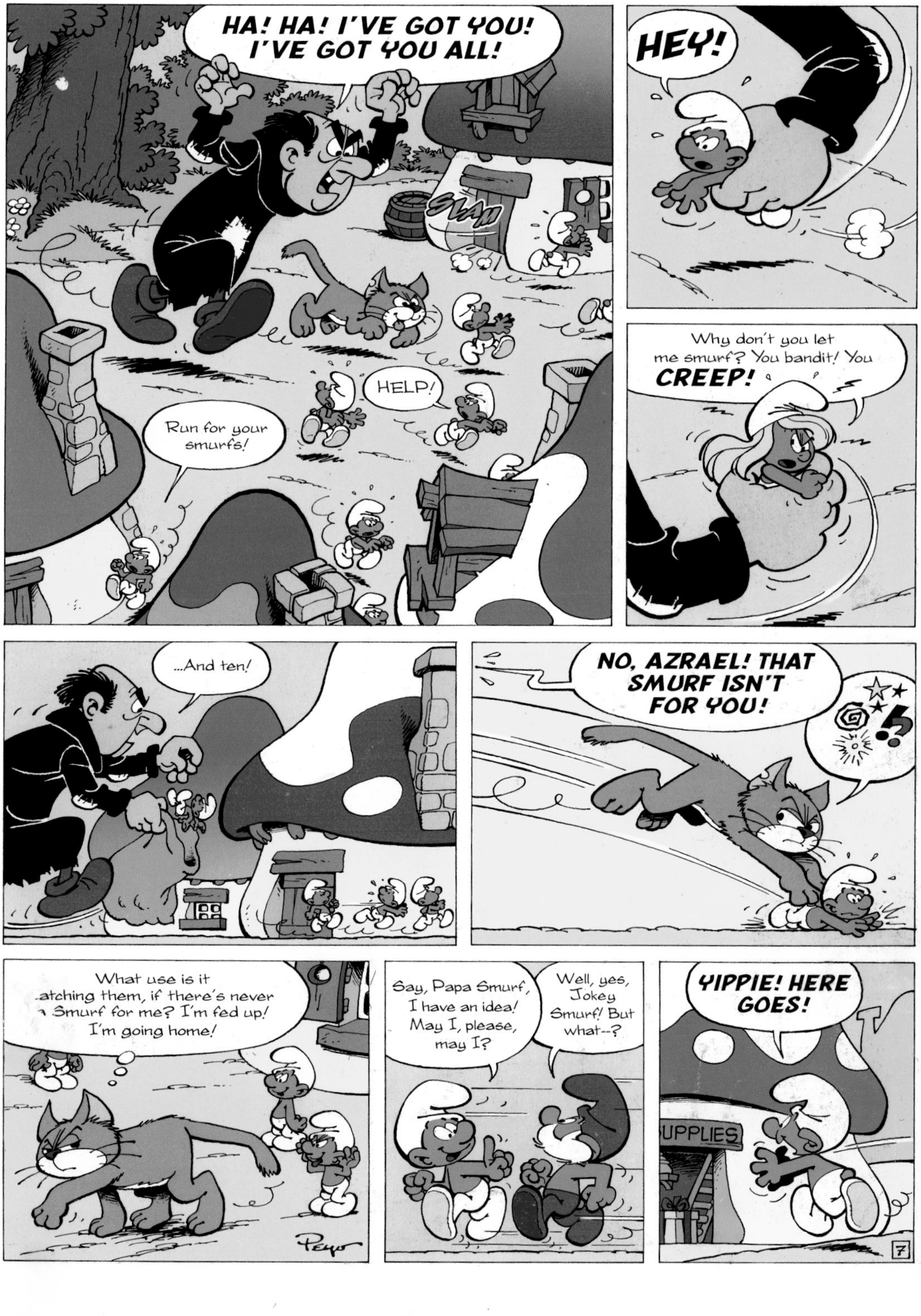

HA! HA! I'VE GOT YOU! I'VE GOT YOU ALL!
SLAM
HELP!
Run for your smurfs!
HEY!
Why don't you let me smurf? You bandit! You CREEP!
...And ten!
NO, AZRAEL! THAT SMURF ISN'T FOR YOU!
What use is it atching them, if there's never Smurf for me? I'm fed up! I'm going home!
Peyo
Say, Papa Smurf, I have an idea! May I, please, may I?
Well, yes, Jokey Smurf! But what--?
YIPPIE! HERE GOES!
UPPLIES
7

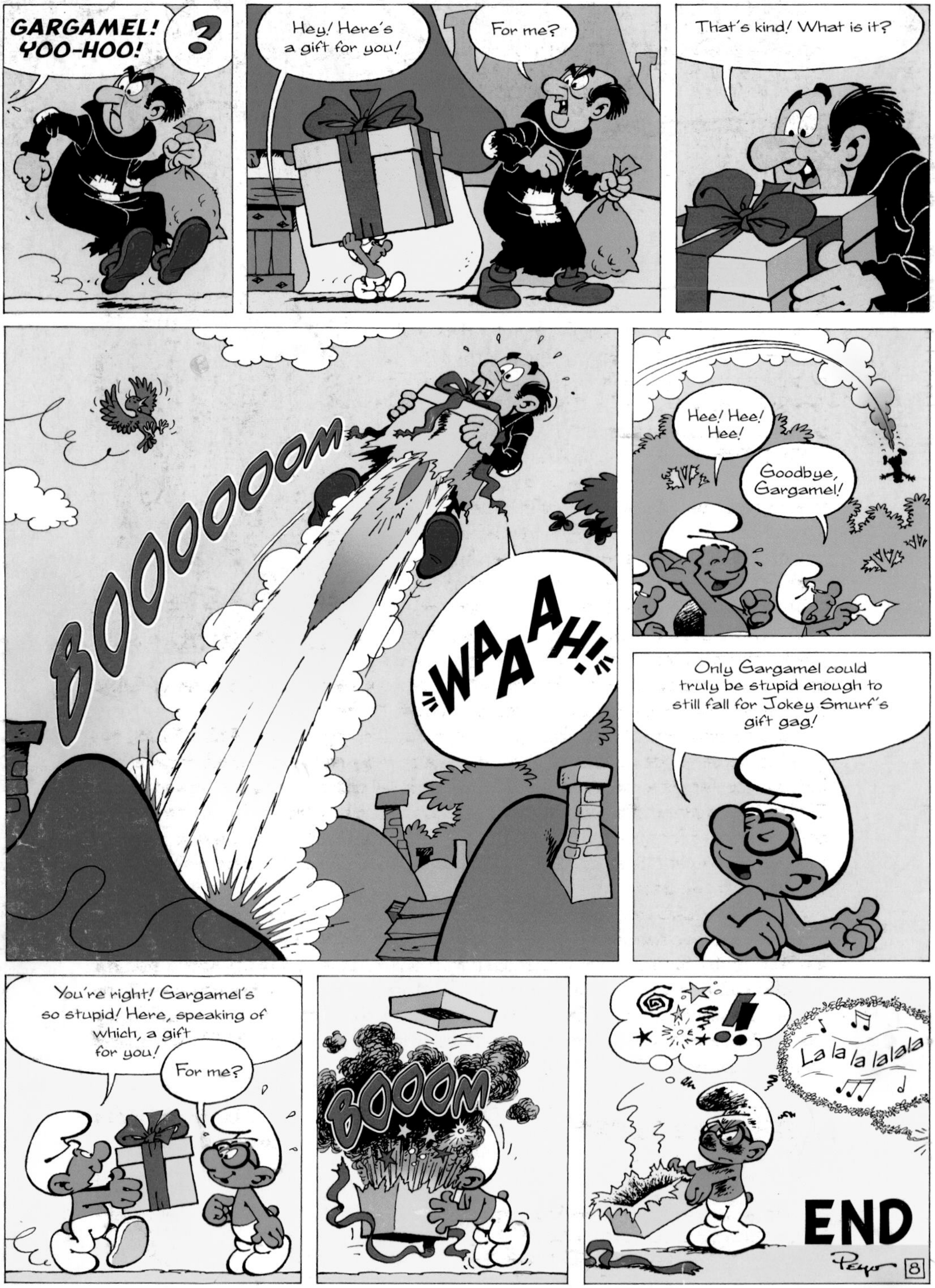
GARGAMEL! YOO-HOO!
?
Hey! Here's a gift for you!
For me?
That's kind! What is it?
BOOOOOOOM
WAAAH!
Hee! Hee! Hee!
Goodbye, Gargamel!
Only Gargamel could truly be stupid enough to still fall for Jokey Smurf's gift gag!
You're right! Gargamel's so stupid! Here, speaking of which, a gift for you!
For me?
BOOOM
La la la lalala
END
Peyo
8

WATCH OUT FOR PAPERCUTZ™

Peyo
the SMURFS
CHRISTMAS
PAPERCUTZ

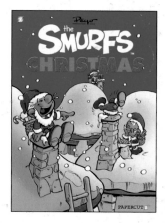

Welcome to the sky-high sixteenth SMURFS graphic novel by Peyo from Papercutz, the Smurf-sized company dedicated to publishing great graphic novels for all ages. I'm Jim Salicrup, the Smurf-in-Chief, with yet another super-smurfy announcement.

Since THE SMURFS #14, I've been telling you that 2013 is the Year of the Smurfs. Aside from the release of SMURFS 2 from Sony Pictures Animation, the ongoing THE SMURFS graphic novel series (available in paperback, hardcover, and special boxed sets), and another FREE COMIC BOOK DAY SMURFS comic, we've added THE SMURFS ANTHOLOGY, a deluxe, large-sized Smurfs series, featuring the Smurfs comics presented in the original publication sequence, as well as the adventures of *Johan and Peewit*, the series that introduced the Smurfs to the world.

We also announced that Papercutz will be publishing BENNY BREAKIRON, the graphic novel series also created by Peyo, starring a super-powered French boy. Indeed, the first volume is available now, and the critics have been raving about BENNY! "It's an exciting moment in American comics when a European creator of such stature is given an entrée to new readership with such careful attention to original artwork and sensitive translation methods," declared Hannah Means-Shannon on *The Beat*.

So, before we're even able to catch our collective breath, would you believe we have yet another special treat to throw your way? It's the perfect way to wind up the Year of the Smurfs—it's THE SMURFS CHRISTMAS! A special all-new collection of holiday Smurf tales! Unlike Jokey Smurfs "gifts," we believe this joyous volume makes a wonderful holiday present—especially for your favorite smurf-loving friends. Whew! Has there ever been a better time to savor THE SMURFS and collect the great comic art classics by Peyo?

STAY IN TOUCH!

EMAIL: Salicrup@papercutz.com
WEB: www.papercutz.com
TWITTER: @papercutzgn
FACEBOOK: PAPERCUTZGRAPHICNOVELS
SNAIL MAIL: Papercutz, 160 Broadway, Suite 700, East Wing, New York, NY 10038

Happy Year of the Smurfs, Blue-Buddies!

Jim

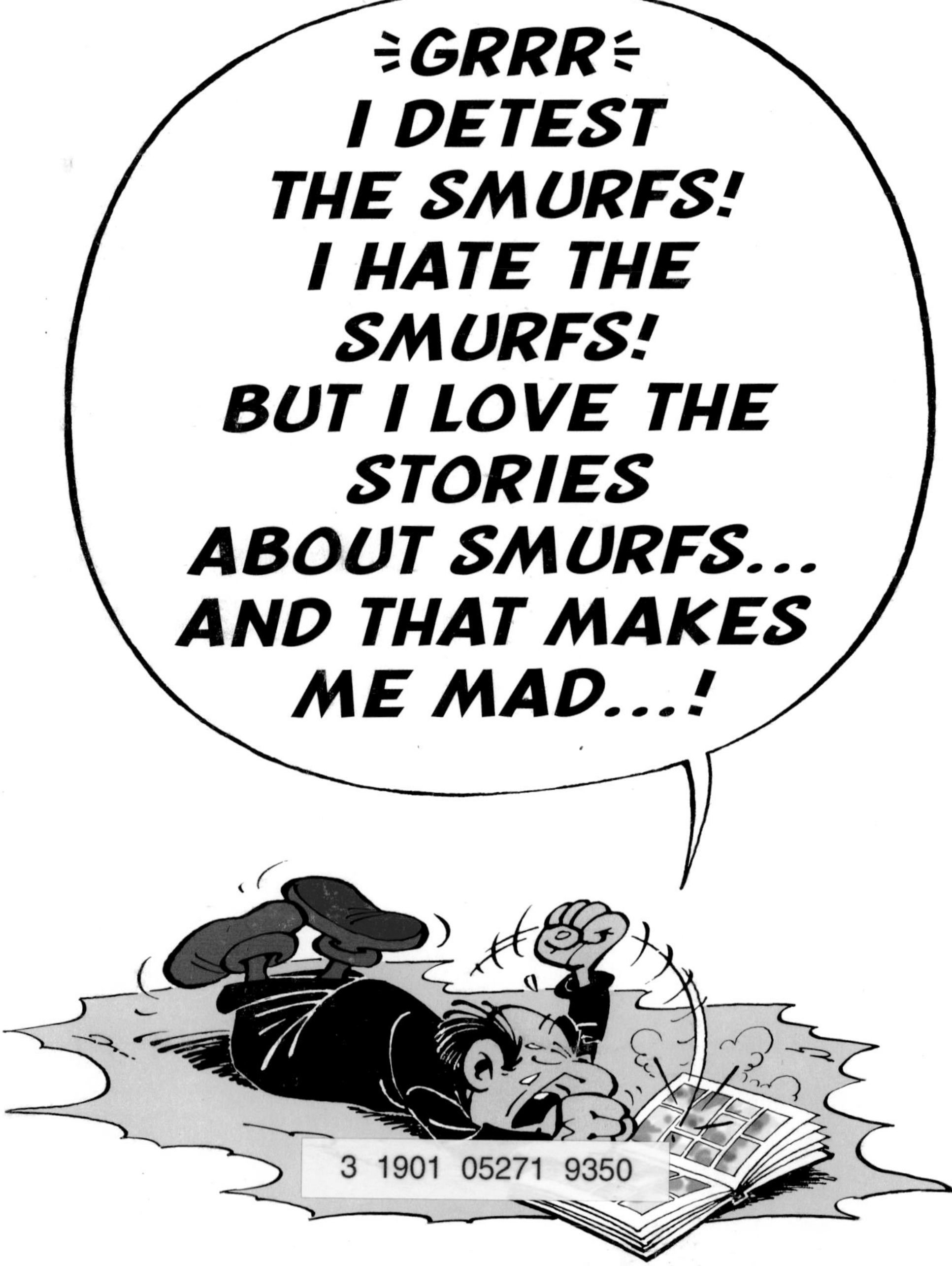
GRRR
I DETEST THE SMURFS! I HATE THE SMURFS! BUT I LOVE THE STORIES ABOUT SMURFS... AND THAT MAKES ME MAD...!